RICK CURL grew up in Kansas City. He received his Bachelor of Arts in English from Benedictine College in Atchison, Kansas and an MBA from Webster University in St. Louis, Missouri. He began writing during his advertising career with AT&T Publishing. He has been an adjunct at the University of Phoenix and was a Midwest voices columnist for the Kansas City Star. He has spoken at the Washington Press Club in Washington D.C. He wrote *Like Two Peas A Father's Memoir* in 2008. He and his wife Ann Simien live in The Village of Loch Lloyd, Mo.

For Jessica and Ashley

PROLOGUE

"A bit chilly out here for an August night, don't you think?" he said bent over, trying to catch his breath, hands resting on his knees, heart racing.

"I suppose that depends on how you like to spend your summer nights. I don't really mind it myself. Fresh air is good for you!" Josh said sarcastically, his gun drawn, the laser sighted 9mm, painted a red dot on the resting man's temple."

"So, what do we do now? he said. He was breathing easier now, but his heart was still racing. "You got the advantage. What do we do now?" he said again.

"Hell, I don't know just yet!" Josh said. "What's the rush? We've been at this for several months now! I was starting to enjoy seeing the country out here just chasing your ass around!"

You don't sound like the fella' I know" He says, turning his face toward Josh.

"You don't know me. You just think you do." Josh answers.

The sun's rays change from a bright yellow to a purple-orange glow as the orb completes its journey across the sky. Evening shadows became one with the night, Waves pound the rocks below like a Greek Chorus chanting a foreboding rhythm. The sharp crack of gunfire is swallowed up by the shrill cries of Seagulls taking wing.

1

It is a late August evening. Sharon, Samantha and Ali are driving home from a weekend of shopping in Chicago. The girls love to go to the city's Michigan Avenue stores with their mother. It's a gorgeous early fall weekend of shopping at some of the best stores and shops Chicago has to offer. Sharon is particularly excited to show Josh the new cocktail dress she bought for the office Christmas party. Sharon and the girls left the Allerton Hotel around eleven o'clock in the morning heading east on interstate 55. They ate breakfast in the hotel before setting out and planned to make a stop in St. Louis to have lunch and more shopping, depending on how things went. Sharon's cell phone chirped. She could see it was Josh calling.

"Hello honey! Are you checking to see if we left the country or something?" teased Sharon.

"Well, no, but maybe I should check the balance on our bank accounts just in case!" Josh chuckled. "How are you ladies doing today? Everything going okay?"

"We're doing just great. We had a wonderful day yesterday and I got a great dress for the party at Marshall Field downtown."

"I thought they were out of business."

"Yeah, it is. It's a Macy's now. I still remember it the old way."

"Mom, let me talk to Dad before you hang up," Ali said softly from the back seat of the SUV. Ali is the youngest of the two girls and loves their dad's attention. This sometimes irritated Savannah as they would often try to outdo the other for Josh's favor.

"Hold on honey, Ali wants to talk to you." said Sharon.

"Hi Dad, you miss me?"

"Of course I do sweetie. Are you and Savannah having a good time?"

"Yes, and I bought you a present, but you can't have it until Christmas." Ali said gleefully. "Savannah got you a present too."

"Hey Ali!" shouted Savannah, "I was going to tell Dad, not you!"

Sharon decided to break up the fuss before it got going, taking the cell phone from Savannah.

"Okay, enough of that. Josh, we just left the hotel about an hour ago. We'll stop in St. Louis for lunch."

"Well I guess I get another free evening to myself." replied Josh.

"Probably so, we won't get home until around five or six this evening."

"Okay, drive safely."

"I'll call you when we leave St. Louis, love you," said Sharon.

As Sharon focused on the road and the few hours ahead, Savannah and Ali are soon lulled into slumber. Sharon turned on the radio, thinking about where they might eat lunch when they get to St. Louis. The highway rolled on through the bright November morning. The sunlight dances across the landscape illuminating the stacks of bailed hay made ready for the winter feeding ahead. Sharon wondered why there were so many Canadian Geese in the fields these days. She remembered when the geese were high in the sky this time of year, flying in almost perfect formation, like a squadron of fighter jets as they begin the journey south to escape the coming winter.

Must be some truth to that global warming thing, she thinks to herself. Sharon looks down at the speedometer and sees the needle pegged at 75. She looks up again just as she passes a sign that tells her they are just thirty miles from St. Louis. Sharon backs off the accelerator a little, the slowing car wakes Ali.

"How much longer, Mom?"

"Just about there."

"I'm hungry," Savannah says with a yawn.

"Well, you guys start thinking about what you want to eat cause' we're pulling into Dodge now." Sharon said.

"I thought we were going to St. Louis." said Savannah, still yawning.

"We are honey, that's just an old expression. Don't you know anything about cowboys?"

"I know about cowboys, but what does Dodge have to do with cowboys, Mom?" Savannah pipped.

"Hey Mom, where is Dodge? Are we there yet!? Said Ali giggling at her own remarks.

"Never mind you two, how about hamburgers and fries for lunch?"

Seated at a table at Steak and Shake, the three ordered burgers, fries, and shakes. Sharon called Josh and let them know they had finished lunch and would soon be heading to Kansas City. Stomachs full, the trio was back in the maroon Ford Explorer and rolling west on I-70. Sharon glanced at the digital clock on the dash. It read 3:04 in the afternoon. She smiled as she watched the girls sleeping in the rearview mirror. Sharon adjusted it to get a clearer view of the road behind. She could see flashing lights of an emergency vehicle speeding down the next hill on the eastbound side of the road. She sees a tractor trailer ahead of the flashing lights. Sharon takes a firm grip on the steering wheel. She could see a Missouri highway patrol car in pursuit. The Ford Explorer reaches the bottom of the hill. Sharon brakes slightly as she approaches another car in her lane. In her rearview mirror she saw another car behind starting to pass. She felt her heart jump as she saw the tractor trailer swaying back and forth across the highway. The swaying began to jerk the cab out of control. At the bottom of the hill the rig broke from the highway and headed across the median directly toward them. And then there was chaos. The rear end of the trailer swung forward, hurtling toward the three cars in a V-shape, like a partially opened straight razor. The driver of the passing car panicked as it passed Sharon. The car swerved and slammed into the red Explorer.

"Oh shit! Sharon yelled as she stood on her brakes to avoid hitting the car in front of her. It didn't matter. The impact of the passing car pushed her off the road anyway. The collision jolted Savannah and Ali out of their nap.

"Momma, what's going on!?" Savannah screamed.

"We're going off the road!" yelled Ali leaning forward in her seat.

"Stay in your seats!" yelled Sharon.

Sharon fought desperately to get the car under control as it plowed across a stream, taking out a freshly strung fence row, plowing through drying corn stalks waiting to be thrashed. She was still fighting for control when the SUV hit a large tree stump, causing it to flip and roll until it came to a sudden stop against a natural wall of stone, erupting into a huge ball of fire about one hundred yards from where Sharon's

SUV came to rest. The other two cars were scooped up by the tractor trailer, grinding and scattering the cars into parts as it plowed across the interstate. Blown tires, glass, mangled metal and luggage lay in witness to the force of uncontrolled weight and velocity. Then there was silence.

When Sharon opened her eyes, she was certain she was waking up from a hard sleep. She was still in her seatbelt as she peered out the shattered windshield. The SUV was upright as Sharon unbuckled her seatbelt, turning around in the seat so she could see the girls.

"What happened Momma?" Savannah said softly. A small trail of blood trickled down her forehead.

"Oh my God Savannah, you're bleeding!" Sharon said frantically. "Ali, are you okay?" Savannah turned her head to look at her sister sitting on the right side of the rear seat. Sharon crawled over the console and into the back seat. She gently shook Ali.

"Ali, Ali, wake up sweetie!"

"Ali isn't moving Momma." Savannah whispered.

2

"Officer John Speight requesting backup at mile marker 114, on interstate 70. Multiple car crash, both east and westbound lanes at risk."

John Speight drove the patrol car in pursuit of the runaway tractor trailer. He maintained enough distance behind the truck as the two vehicles roared down that steep hill into the valley at almost ninety per miles hour. A forty-thousand-pound vehicle operates at great risk at that speed. The driver eventually slowed the truck, pulled to the side of the road and stopped.

Josh and Bill were having a couple beers at an old beer establishment in the Waldo section of the city when Josh got the call from Officer Speight.

"I gotta' go. Sharon and the girls have been in an accident."

"Oh crap", said Bill. "Where are you going?"

"To where the accident is!"

Josh jumped off the barstool and bolted outside, stopping on the sidewalk. Bill dropped a twenty-dollar bill on the table and followed him out.

"Listen, I don't think it's a good idea for you to drive," Said Bill. "You're really upset."

"Then you take me. You drive!"

"Okay, I can take you. Maybe you should call that policeman back and find out if an ambulance has arrived yet. If it has, we could just go straight to the hospital. Otherwise, we might wind up passing them going the other way."

Josh made the phone call. Sharon and Savannah were in two ambulances heading toward Kansas City. Bill and Josh arrived at the hospital just as the ambulances arrived at the emergency entrance. Bill stopped the car as Josh jumped out and ran toward the ambulance. The EMT's opened the doors and rushed Sharon and Savannah into the hospital. Josh ran beside the two gurneys as they raced through the doors. He could see Sharon and Savannah's battered faces, eye's swollen shut, their faces puffy and bruised. One of the doctor's grabbed Josh by the arm.

"It's going to be quite a while before we get them stabilized. We have a private room you could use to if you like."

"That might be a good deal Josh." Bill said.

"It's just down the hall a bit. Follow me and I'll show you where it is. I'm Dr. Reynolds, you're Mr. Landry?"

"Yes, I'm Josh Landry and this is my friend Bill Haus.

"I'm sorry about what happened to your family. We will do our best for them. Can I get you and your friend some coffee or something?"

"That would be fine, thanks," said Josh.

"I'll have someone from the staff to bring something for you both. I need to attend to your family now."

The doctor smiled and gently closed the door to the room. Josh was standing, fidgeting with his cell phone.

"Why don't you sit down and try to relax a bit Josh? Dr. Reynolds looks like a smart doctor. Sharon and Savannah will be fine in his hands. I can see it in his eyes. You know…he has that confident look." Bill paused. Josh looked up, nodding his head.

"Thanks Bill, you always know what to say."

"That recliner looks real comfy. If you don't stretch out on it, I will." Bill said.

The door opened and a young nurse walked in pushing a little cart of a few cans of assorted soft drinks, bottled water, and coffee. She was an attractive woman of olive complexion. Her long, jet black hair pulled back behind her ears flowed down her back.

"Hello, I'm Tasha. I work with Dr. Reynolds. Help yourselves to the refreshments. Can I help you with anything else?"

"Do you know anything about my little girl?" asked Josh.

"Your daughter is still in the emergency room."

"No, I mean…" Josh stopped, his voice cracked.

"He wants to know about Ali, his other daughter." said Bill.

"I'm so sorry, Mr. Landry. I really don't have any information about her. But I'll try to find out something for you, okay? I'll be back later to check on you." Tasha smiled and left the two in the room. Josh watched her walk down the long, shiny hallway until she disappeared through a pair of double doors.

"I can hang out with you if you like Josh", said Bill.

"That's okay Bill. I know you probably need to get back to your business. I'm going to be here awhile, so you go ahead."

"Okay, call me when you get a chance and let me know how things are going."

Bill left the room and Josh settled into the recliner. He could hear Bill's footsteps as he walked down the hall. Josh closed his eyes, thinking of his grandfather.

"Slow down a bit Josh, save your energy."
Josh heard his grandfather yelling at him from across the pasture. Josh loved to run as a boy. His grandfather ran track too in his youth. He and Josh were close. Josh remembered his

family going to the farm during spring break in the bayou country of southern Louisiana. He was running track in high school then. His grandfather wanted to share some of his own experience with his young grandson while he was visiting. It was a great time for both. Josh could feel his heartbeat climbing as he ran. He loved to run. It gave him a sort of freedom, a release from some of the unpleasant sounds of life. It was bliss. He felt lighter than air. Josh remembered the sun's rays glinting off the blades of grass. The wind swept across his face carrying the fresh smell of water from the little fishing pond behind the barn. He could almost taste it.

"Breathe deeper Josh," his grandfather would say. That voice was the only thing Josh could hear when he ran.

"Good, now extend your stride a little. Cover more ground that way."

Now Josh could feel no pain. He remembered how it felt when the heart, lungs and blood are all trying to get the body moving. He moved past the heart rate climb and felt it all level out in harmony. A rhythm when all the body functions achieve the sensation of going on forever.

"Okay, Josh that's enough. We don't want to push too hard."

"Mr. Landry?"

The sound of Tasha's voice interrupted Josh's daydreaming. He sat up in the chair as she came through the door.

"I came to tell you that your wife and daughter are resting well. You can see them if you like, but they are both under sedation. It will be a few hours before the grogginess wears off."

"I'd like to see them now. Can we do that, Tasha?"

"Of course, just follow me. We are going to the fourth, intensive care unit. They will be moved to a regular hospital room in a day or two."

Josh followed the Tasha out the door and down the long gleaming hall to the hospital lobby elevators. She pressed the up button and the door opens. Josh holds the door for Tasha and steps in behind her.

'The newscasts are saying that a highway patrol car was chasing a truck," said Tasha. "But they don't say much else."

Josh looked at her a moment and paused. Tasha sensed his hesitation.

"I still haven't heard anything about Ali." She said.

"That's okay Tasha. I appreciate your concern," Josh replied. "My phone has a few messages on it I haven't listened to. Maybe one of them will tell me something."

Tasha nodded. The elevator door opened, and Tasha led Josh to the room where Sharon and Savannah lie bruised and bandaged. Josh stood in front of their beds, looking at them.

"If you need anything Mr. Landry, I will be here on the floor for a while longer." Said Tasha.

"Thanks, I'm going to be here for a while."

"Stay as long as you like. I can get blankets and a pillow if you decide to stay. I'll check on you just before my shift ends." Tasha smiled and closed the door.

3

Delores awoke to the smell of fresh roasted coffee beans and the warmth of sunlight streaming through the freshly starched linen curtains bordering the bedroom window of the little cottage. She and Jason loved the Cayman Islands. Jason enjoyed his ritual of sitting on the deck in the morning sun reading the *Cayman Compass*, taking in the smell of the Caribbean Sea. Delores turned over in the bed and saw a cup of coffee waiting for her on the nightstand. She pulls on an old sweatshirt, slips on her flipflops and walks out to the deck.

"Morning, what's in the news today?"

Delores walks over to the deck rail next to her husband and gently rubs his neck.

"Oh, nothing special, I guess, just some political stuff. Seems our government is having some sort of a scandal or something," said Jason. "Did you sleep okay?"

"I slept okay I guess," Delores yawned. "I woke up in the middle of the night thinking about Rene and everybody back home."

"Yeah, I know. Have you talked to Rene lately? The last I spoke with her was about four days ago."

"I plan to give her a call today around her lunchtime," said Delores. "She's probably busy at work. I think I worry too much sometimes. What's on your agenda today?"

'Not much. I need to go to the bank and then get a haircut. Think I'm going to skip the workout this morning," replied Jason. "What about you?'

"Well, after I call Rene, I suppose I'll just piddle around here until you get back. Let's plan something for this evening. I heard there's a good little combo playing at one of the little hotspots in town."

"Okay, let's do that," said Jason, looking up from the newspaper.

"Maybe we should invite everyone out here soon."

"Everyone like who?" said Jason.

"Our daughter Rene of course, and Sharon, Madeline, and Josh and Sharon and the girls."

"Sounds like a good idea", said Jason.

The little television on the deck table flashes a breaking news banner across the screen. A news reporter stands on the courthouse steps of one of the old Georgetown judicial buildings. Jason and

Delores watch as Prime Minister Brandon Lockett and his political rival Jonathan Hatch spar over the latest accusation by Hatch that the Prime Minister was abusing his power. Hatch goes further inferring Lockett was also failing in his leadership regarding his policy on trade. In the mid 90's, Lockett worked as an international trade lobbyist for the British government. His specialty included global marketing and transportation. Lockett came to power because of his diplomacy within the Caribbean islands and the British Crown.

"You can tell it's getting close to election time", said Delores. "I kind of like our Prime Minister."

"Me too," Jason replied. "That Johnathan Hatch guy is full of crap."

"Well let's hope it all works out. As for me, I think I will go down to that little boutique I found near the beach and see if they have any new stuff."

"Enjoy your day," smiles Jason, nodding. "Think about where you want to go tonight while you are out."

Delores heard her cell phone ring. She runs back into the cottage to get it. The caller ID identifies the caller.

"Hello Josh! We were just talking about you and Sharon!"

"Hey Delores, how are you and Jason?" said Josh, softly.

"We're fine, it's good to hear from you," Delores pauses. "You sound a little different. Are you feeling well? Is everything alright?"

"Not really."

4

The sun seemed to rise earlier than usual on the day of the funeral for Ali. It was a warm September. A nearly cloudless sky honored her passing. No rain in the forecast. Jason and Delores helped the many friends and relatives sign the guestbook, while Bill and Rene stayed close to Josh and Sharon in the receiving line.

"How are you guys holding up?" Bill whispers to Josh.

"I'm not sure how I feel." Josh replied.

Bill smiled softly at Sharon. He walks over, takes her hand and kisses her on the cheek. The funeral was simple. At least four hundred friends, classmates, neighbors, family members and media came to say goodbye to Ali and support Sharon and Josh.

Father Bob Steward, a devout and soft-spoken man and close friend of the family delivers kind words. The Catholic priest did his best to bring consolation to everyone in the room, avoiding as he could not to repeat the many clichés heard during times of grief and sorrow. After the service, mourners mingled in the lobby of the church. Most of them trying to catch up on old friendships and recounting memories slowly drifting way in the quickly passing years.

A tall silver-haired man in a dark suit opened the doors of the limousine parked under the canopy of the funeral home. Josh held Sharon's' hand as they walk toward the car.

"I didn't know your daughter ma'am, but my heart aches for your loss", said the tall man. "I too, know this grief."

Sharon noted the quiet serenity in his voice. She pulls the black veil away from her and touches him gently on the back of his hand, then steps into the limo. Josh, Savannah and the rest of the family follow. A lone cloud covers the late morning sun marking the moment. A procession follows the black limo as it moves slowly along the trail meandering through the cemetery to Ali's resting place.

5

Josh spends the next few days helping Sharon and Savannah heal from the injuries suffered in the crash. This morning Josh awakes and sits up in the bed. He looks over at Sharon, still sleeping. Savannah is asleep in her room. Jason and Delores are spending a few more days with daughter Rene.

"Josh Landry investigations is not going to investigate by itself." Josh thinks to himself. "Time to get back to work."

Josh slips quietly out of bed, not wanting to disturb Sharon, walks into the bathroom, closing the door. He brushes his teeth. In the bathroom mirror Josh sees the wear of the days in his face. His eyes not as bright, crow's feet in the corners. He turns on the shower, pulls off his pajama pants and steps in. The warmth of the water flows over his body. He remembers a client he needs to follow up with. Anton Garibaldi has a daughter he wants to reconnect with. Josh had promised to help him just before the crash. It wasn't the kind of investigative work he like to take on, but the old gentleman was insistent. He got a reference about Josh from one of his friends who retired as Chief of the Kansas City Police. Josh was a detective in the department a few years back. Josh steps out of the shower and grabs a large blue towel from the linen closet. Sharon always kept the towels neatly arranged. Josh appreciated this small comforted. He steps back into the bedroom.

"Where are you off to this morning?" Sharon said, yawning.

"No more regular paychecks from the Department, so JL Investigations is now open for business!" Josh said, trying to spark some morning humor. "How are you feeling this morning?"

"Okay, I guess." Sharon said softly, pulling her hair back. "I've got a doctor appointment later this morning."

"With your regular doctor?"

"No, with my psychologist. "

"Is it helping?" queries Josh.

"I don't know, I guess it helps some." Helps me get my work done."

"Maybe you should change doctors, maybe get a different point of view might help," said Josh.

"Don't worry about it, Josh. I've got a handle on it!" snapped Sharon. Josh was caught off guard. Tucking his shirt into his pants, he turned and looked at her. Sharon looked at him, then looked away. "I'm sorry. That came out wrong."

"That's okay. I was just trying to help. Maybe you should take some more time off work," said Josh. "We could take a short vacation somewhere, or you and Savannah could go visit your mother."

"Maybe, I was thinking maybe I would stay with my Mom for a while. I'm probably not being fair to you right now." said Sharon. Josh paused then sits on the bed next to Sharon.

"If that makes you feel better, I'm all for it. Let's talk about it some more later. I need to get to work. I'll be home around dinner time." Said Josh. "Just thinking, what about Savannah? She doesn't need any more stress."

"She can come with me or stay here with you. Whatever makes her more comfortable." It won't be forever. I just need some me time." Her voice trailed off.

"Sometimes healing medicine has a bitter taste." Said Josh.

6

Joshua sits in the small kitchen of his suburban Kansas City home sipping his first cup of coffee. It is a cold late November morning. The Holiday season is about to begin, and Thanksgiving is just a few days away. The television in the background opens the day with its routine schedule of the latest morning news events of the last twenty-four hours. Josh unrolls the morning newspaper and scans the front page. The morning news anchor verify the headlines. He knows the next hour or so would really be a mix of entertainment and news events, so he would not waste his morning with chatter about another diet sensation or some hotshot celebrity of marginal talent clamoring for attention.

"Morning Daddy, did you remember to get some milk?"

"Morning sweetie, yeah I remembered. It's in the fridge. Did you sleep okay?"

"I slept fine, but I wish it was Saturday again," Savannah yawned. Savannah is a high school senior, busy with the business of graduating from high school and preparing for college.

"Saturday will be here soon enough. "You better get ready for school. "Your mother will be here to pick you up in another thirty minutes."

"I know Dad, I'll be ready as usual. What's the big deal?" she piped.

"The big deal is that your mom will read me the riot act if you walk out of this house looking like anything but a princess. You know that and I'm sure you don't want your very best friend, namely me, in the doghouse with your mom, right?"

Savannah paused on the stairway and gave Josh that little concurring smile as she sprints up the stairs.

The television drones on in the background while Josh opens his laptop and begins checking his emails and his calendar for the days' commitments. He quickly sees he doesn't have anything scheduled until later in the day. He decides to go to the gym first and then head on to the office. As Josh pours himself a coffee refill, he hears a car pulling in the driveway and the accompanying turbo whine of Sharon's black Porsche Carrera. She usually honks and waits for Savannah to come out, but this morning, she decides to ring the doorbell and walk into the house. Savannah walks briskly down the stairs and sees her mother standing in the foyer.

"Morning Mom, you didn't have to get out of the car, I'm ready to go!" Sharon hugs her daughter then gives her an "inspection", smiling as Savannah executes a little ballerina turn.

Josh comes in from the kitchen as the two ladies are laughing. He comes to military style attention and slaps a salute.

"Well, does she pass inspection ma'am?" Josh asks. Sharon eyes Josh and smiles.

"I think so, at ease soldier." Sharon looks at Savannah. "We better get going if I'm going to get you to school in time! Josh gives them each a peck on the cheek and watched as they get into the Porsche, back out of the driveway and drive away.

"Mom, are we still going shopping tomorrow? I still have to get Dad a present for Christmas."

"That's the plan dear. What are you going to get him?" The Porsche whines as Sharon downshifts and slows to exit interstate 435.

I think I'm going to get him some new earbuds. Maybe the Bluetooth ones. He keeps leaving his old ones in his workout shorts and washes them in with everything else!"

"That sounds like a good idea," said Sharon.

"I thought so too," Savannah says with a smile. "Besides, the technology has improved. Time for a new one!"

"Okay dear, we're here." Sharon quickly maneuvers the Porsche into the school drive and pulls up to the curb. She stops the car barely five feet from the bumper of a white Chevy Tahoe, like a gymnast dismounting from a routine on the balance beam. Savannah pops out of the car, grabbing her backpack and the little hand painted flowered purse Sharon brought her from a shopping trip somewhere. She was always bringing Savannah something.

"Don't forget Mom, I'm going to the basketball game tonight with some of my friends!" Savannah yells as she closes the door.

"I remember, call me when you get out of school today." Sharon pulls away from the curb and out of the schoolyard. She steers the Porsche toward Corporate Woods business park and makes a right turn onto Indian Creek Parkway. A phone call comes in through the car audio. Sharon can see the call is from Rene', Sharon's administrative assistant.

"Good morning, Rene!"

"Hi, Sharon, where are you?" asked Rene'.

"I'm in the parking lot. What's up?"

"Oh, nothing pressing. Your mother called. I told her you were on the phone with a client, so she wouldn't worry."

"Thanks Rene, I'll call her as soon as I get in."

Sharon pulls the car into her regular parking space, grabs the leather case from the rear seat and walks briskly across the parking lot toward the three-story brick and glass building nestled in a heavily shaded corner of the wooded corporate neighborhood of both private and corporate business headquarters. Sharon enters the shiny glass revolving doors and steps onto the pristine, polished white marble floor. She walks a little more cautiously, thinking how embarrassed she would be if she slips and falls in her high heels. Next time I will remember to wear flat shoes! She says to herself.

Reaching the top of the escalator, Sharon walks into the ladies' restroom to do a last check of her makeup. She exits and walks a few steps down the hall to the offices of Cavanaugh International Sharon, opens the huge glass door and walks to the reception area. The brightly lit room seems to radiate with energy as light beams down through a large portal in the ceiling. The décor is modern but invitingly comfortable. At the rear of the room is a large counter with two people, a young man and woman busily chatting on the phone and punching a computer screen. Hovering on the wall behind them is a Holographic image of Earth floating in space. Directly below the hologram, Cavanaugh International appears in distinct gold script.

"Good morning Sharon", says the young woman looking up from her computer.

"Good morning Jill", Sharon replies. "We still need to do happy hour sometime soon."

"I'm ready when you are!" Jill answers.

"How about next Wednesday? Get back to me and let me know. I gotta' run. Rene is waiting for me I'm sure!" Sharon walks past the copy room and sees Rene sorting through a stack of mail.

"Hi Rene, anything in there for me?" Sharon asks.

"Not much, just a letter from your law school."

"Probably from the alumnus asking for support for new students or something." Sharon said. "Anything else?"

"No, but Dave Cavanaugh wants to have a meeting later today," Said Rene.

"What time does he want to meet?" asked Sharon.

Two o'clock. I already checked your schedule and I told him you are open." Rene said. I assume you still are."

"Of course, he is the boss. I was going to meet with the office maintenance chief about some IT stuff, but I can move it. What else you got for me?"

"That's it, oh wait, I forgot. A Warren James wants you to call. He didn't say what it was about. That's his number on the memo I put on your desk," Said Rene.

"Okay, I'll call him later. Give me a few minutes, I'm going to call mom back, before things get too busy. Then I will call Warren James", said Sharon. She walks into her office behind Rene's desk and sets her briefcase on the chair facing the desk.

"Running a little late today?" said Maddie.

"Just a little bit. Good morning mother."

"Did you get my granddaughter to school on time? You know I haven't seen Savannah in a long time now. When is she coming to see me? We've got some shopping to do."

"Mom, you and Savannah just went shopping two weeks ago!" Sharon says laughing."

"Are you sure? Couldn't be, anyway, we still have some unfinished stuff to do."

"You and Savannah always have some unfinished stuff to do. After you get finished with her, she won't want to do anything for herself! Anyway, Mom, I've got to go. I have a meeting later today and I haven't don't anything yet."

"Okay, call me later," said Maddie.

"Okay, I will, Bye."

7

David Cavanaugh stood in his office looking across the parking lot at the uniform and perfect setting of an urban forest of well-manicured trees and shrubbery. He admired the union of nature's creation and man's need to organize. In the distance, he could see I-435 and observes the elaborate concrete and steel roadway system expanding as the city continues its quiet growth and evolution from a Cowtown to a major metro of over two million people. Cavanaugh International was founded as a charitable foundation with the mission of assisting people and causes which otherwise could not exist. It also acts as a consultant to other organizations needing extraordinary assistance. Cavanaugh International is now so successful it was receiving requests for assistance from all over the world. Today, David got a call from an organization in the Cayman Islands consulting the Governor on a matter "of great importance", according to the Governor's communique. The desk phone buzzes. He turns his gaze across KC and reaches for the instrument on his desk.

"Hi Sharon, you still got time to talk?"

Of course, David, you want to meet in your office?

"How about I come to your place…office I mean?" David said with a chuckle.

David and Sharon worked well together, and he had grown very fond of her. Sometimes he bordered on flirting, but always kept it professional.

"Sure, come on down."

"Be there in ten minutes. I promise not to take up your entire afternoon".

David could talk for hours if it is something, he is passionate about. Sharon is his favorite audience.

8

Josh searches his closet looking for something warm to wear. He finds his old high school sweater tucked deep in the back under an old hooded sweatshirt. Smiling, Josh pulls the sweater out for a better look. He reflects on the days when he imagined himself a major league player. Josh kept himself in good shape and played sports all during high school. He wasn't an imposing figure, but he was always fit. He played baseball during high school until he lost a front tooth to a high fly ball in center field which he lost in the sun. Josh neglected to protect his face as he guessed the flight of the ball. The busted lip healed; the wonders of cosmetic dentistry patched up his smile. After that, he began to flinch at that hard sphere thrown with great speed. He played a little in college but realized he just didn't have "enough stuff" and decided to move on with his plans for a career outside of sports.

Not enough stuff, he thought to himself as he hung the sweater back on the hanger and placed it back in the corner of the closet. Josh packed his workout bag and headed out to the garage where a maroon Buick LaCrosse and a black 67' Camaro sat, waiting to be chosen. Most days Josh took the Buick to work, but today he would take the Camaro".

I feel like the Camaro today, he thought to himself. His cell phone rings. The caller ID announcing it's Bill.

"Morning Bill." Josh answers walking toward the Camaro.

"Hey Josh, you still coming to the gym today?"

"On my way now. Should be there in about 15."

"Okay, see you then."

Josh opens the door of the Camaro and slides under the wheel. He turns the ignition and the perfect sound of three hundred and nine-six cubic inches of old school V8 thunder into life. Josh backs out of the garage. An empty beer bottle, jarred by the vibration of raw horsepower, crashes from Josh's tool bench onto the garage floor. He decides to clean up the glass when he returns. He pulls into the street heading in the same direction Sharon and Savannah went just an hour or so earlier. Fifteen minutes later he was in the locker room of the gym. Josh quickly changes into his gym clothes, throws his gym bag into his locker closes the door and walks into the gym.

"What's up Josh Landry?"

It's the booming, always happy with Life voice of Bill Haus, Josh's best friend. He and Josh spent many hours working out together and just talking about sports and life for Josh after the crash. Bill was always at the gym, or so it seemed, and Josh always looked forward to seeing him there.

Hey Bill, how you doing man?!" Josh answers. "Time to get this workout in. After this, I'm headed for the office. Business good?"

Trying to stay afloat, but things have been pretty good lately." Bill added, "if you don't talk about the cost of jet fuel!

Bill grew up in western Kansas on the plains in the triangle between Dodge City, Garden City and Liberal. His parents owned a water well drilling company when he was a kid. The farmland out there is flat and dry for as far as you can see, so searching for water for area farmers is big business. Bill, a big, rugged, handsome guy of German descent learned to fly small aircraft and started a crop-dusting service. The business gave way to a move to Kansas City and the birth of Jet Stream, a leasing operation catering to corporate and private users.

"So, you and Sharon still keeping two households? Bill asked, "I hope you don't mind me asking."

Yeah, for now, till we get some things worked. It's been hard for both of us." Josh paused, "Hey, don't you still owe me a drink from that time we all went out after that wedding reception you hosted at one of the hangers?"

"Yep, when you want to go have some fun again? We need to slow down and catch up!" said Bill.

"Well, call me later and let's see if we can hook up somewhere for a couple of martinis or something," replied Josh,

"I've got to get to the office and catch up on the phone calls."

"Okay, I've got a meeting with a guy from Talon LLC about setting up a couple of my Citations." Bill said.

"Setting them up?" asked Josh.

"Yeah, this company does armament and stuff for limos, planes, etc."

"Wow, are you expecting trouble?"

No, but lately potential clients ask if my planes are armed. I don't know, maybe the Somali pirate thing and all that other stuff has everybody a little jittery."

"I know what you mean. Okay Bill, I'm heading out now."

"I want to hit the steam room first. I'll give you a call later." Said Bill. "Hey Josh…"

"Yeah?"

"If you need any help with anything, be sure and let me know. Jean and I really miss hanging out with you guys like we used to."

Josh smiled and nodded appreciatively. He turned and walked out of the locker room, into the busy lobby towards his car. He thought about how quickly things have changed in the last five years.

9

Sharon and Rene were busy going over some of the day's activity when David Cavanaugh tapped on the frame of the door of Sharon's office.

"Hey ladies, you two sure look busy with something. Can I help?"

"Oh, hi David, come on in. Rene and I are just going over the planner for next month. You have something you want to put on it?"

"I might. We *are* an international company!"

"I will leave you two to your business," says Rene softly. She gathers her papers and slips out the door."

David Cavanaugh takes a bottle of Dasani from the small fridge sitting in the corner of Sharon's office and makes himself comfortable in one of the two cushy calfskin leather chairs sitting in the rear of her office. An interesting little table sat between the two chairs and an imposing rendition of *Hannibal of Carthage* hung on the wall directly behind. Sharon takes a seat in the other chair. She notices David studying it.

"A friend of Josh's gave him that portrait when Josh decided to leave the police force, but we never found a place for it. He said I could hang it wherever I liked, so I brought it here."

"A bit too much testosterone for such a lovely lady, isn't it?" says David.

"Probably, but it presents a different spin on some of our gentlemen clients when they come in here." Sharon replies. "I think it is to our advantage. Besides, it is a nice piece of art if nothing else." David sets his Dasani on the little table and sits up and slightly forward in his chair.

"Sharon, I've been contacted by the diplomatic liaison for the Prime Minister of the Cayman Islands."

"Really, so what do they need us to do for them?"

"Well, as yet I am not exactly sure, but it concerns some political damage control of sorts and something to do with international shipping, trucking in particular."

"Brandon Lockett is the Governor of the Caymans," says Sharon, googling her iPhone.

"Correct, and he wants to meet with us." Sharon smiles, realizing she might get to visit Delores and Jason and conduct some serious business."

"Okay, that sounds easy enough. How much information do we want to get?"

David sits back again in the Chair and finishes the bottled of Dasani.

"The usual stuff. Try to get the info down to specific individuals in the Cayman government who have influence on outcomes. You know, the lobbyists, politicians with interest in the trade arena, etc."

"Got it, and how soon do we need this info?" Sharon looks up from her notetaking.

"Well, they sounded pretty anxious, but we have some time to finish up on this month's business before we have to get started."

"So, about two or three weeks then?" said Sharon.

"I think so and you need to arrange travel there. I won't be going initially. I told them you would make the first face to face contact. I will join you on the second meeting." David stood up and stretched.

Rene pops back in the door.

So, it looks like we got some work to do!" Rene says with a giggle. Rene was always busy. She's the kind of person who just can't sit still. One of her best assets. Rene could work for hours researching the minutest detail.

"Oh, before I forget, a Warren James called.... says he's called before, but you haven't returned his call."

"Thanks Rene, I'll call him before I leave today. In the meantime, we need to start digging up dirt for the Governor of the Caymans!" Sharon walks behind her desk, picks up the phone and remembers she doesn't have the little notepad paper Rene had just given her   "Rene, could you get Warren James on the phone for me? I misplaced that darn little note you gave me."

A few moments later, Rene walks into Sharon's office with a remote phone in hand.

"Warren James is on the line for you Sharon." Rene handed the phone to her.

"Hello, this is Sharon Landry.

"Good afternoon Mrs. Landry, it is good to finally hear your voice. I've been trying to reach you for some time now."

"I must apologize for taking so long to return your call. How can I help you now that we have finally connected?"

"I understand your husband does a pretty good job in the private investigation business." Warren James spoke in a low calculating voice that made Sharon uncomfortable.

"Well, I suppose he does. If you need investigative work, I can give you the contact number to his office." Rene said.

"Mrs. Landry, it is my understanding that you and your husband are separately investigating the accident which took your daughter's life. We would like to work with you on that, if you find that agreeable."

"Exactly who is we, Mr. James?" Sharon was getting a little agitated with this stranger who spoke about things so personal to her."

"I represent Teamsters International. I was hoping we might be able to meet privately. What do you think?"

Sharon paused for a moment. Josh was investigating the facts of the crash under the radar and on his own time, while the police and everyone else churned out a circus of paperwork on the matter. It was time consuming work and Josh had paying clients to keep happy at the same time. He might be interested in a little help she thought.

"I am curious Mr. James. I will discuss this with my husband," said Sharon. "One of us will get back to you. Do I have your proper contact information?"

"Yes, you do."

'I will get back to you shortly, Mr. James."

"That will be fine, Mrs. Landry. It's been a pleasure talking to you."

"Goodbye, Mr. James."

She still didn't like that voice.

10

Josh thinks about his family as he drives across the Broadway bridge in the north side of downtown Kansas City. The bridge crosses over to the old Kansas City Municipal Airport which thrived during the days when Trans World Airlines, Braniff and Pan Am were the heavy lifters. The original terminal still stands but is now an exhibition facility for aircraft related activities. Surrounding the airport are several hangers and offices housing private and small business commercial aircraft. Josh presses the button on his cell phone to call Bill Haas.

"Hey Josh, what's up?"

"I'm downtown, thought I would drop by for a few minutes if you're not too busy.

"Sure, come on by. I got something to show you." Bill replied.

Josh drove down the strip, passing several hangers of small aircraft until he spots the *Jet Stream* sign marking the entrance. He guns the engine before turning the ignition off, closed the door and walked into the brightly lit office. From the entrance, Josh could immediately see Bill's office in the back corner. There was a comfortable reception area furnished with a couple of designer chairs and a low, long glass topped table accented with a chrome lining and supported by a frame of ebony and a distinct ivory trim. A receptionist greets him as Josh walks into the area.

"Good morning sir, can I help you?" said a cheery voice with a smiling face.

"Good morning, I came to see Bill Haas." Said Josh.

"You must be his friend Josh, right?" said the lady with the cheery voice, still smiling.

"That's me." Said Josh.

"Follow me, and I'll show you to the way."

The lady with the smiling face walked briskly to the back of the office toward a large metal door marked *Caution Authorized Personnel Only.* She grabbed the door handle and the door opened onto the hangar area where two Citation jet aircraft stood, poised and ready.

"There's Pete over there," she said pointing the way. "He'll take you from here."

"Thanks for your help miss...."

"Connie."

"Thanks Connie." Josh watched for a moment as Connie walked back to the front.

"Afternoon sir, can I help you with something?" The man had a rugged, solid face. He was wearing a green ball cap with the *Jet Stream* logo emblazoned across the front.

"Hi, I was just admiring these beautiful planes. Are you Pete?"

"Yes, I'm Pete, Pete Johnson." He took off his glove to shake Josh's hand. I'm the pilot/technician around here, something like a first mate of sorts. "You must be Bill's friend.

Josh shook his hand.

"Watch out Pete, that's a dangerous man you're talkin' to." Josh would recognize that booming voice anywhere. It was Bill walking briskly across the shining concrete floor toward the two men."

"Josh and I were just getting acquainted," said Pete.

"Sorry, to keep you waiting Josh. I was working with some fellows looking to lease a plane."

"That's okay Bill. You've got to take care of business first." Josh turned toward one the *Citations*. "Man, those babies look awesome!"

"Yea, they are pretty cool. C'mon Pete, let's you and me give Josh a close up look."

The three men walked across the concrete floor of the hanger toward one of the two planes. Josh noticed the planes immediate aerodynamic beauty, but most noticeable was the gleam of the plane's exterior.

"I don't think I've ever seen a plane so shiny', said Josh.

"Pete does a great job keeping them looking good. It's a selling tool when a prospective client comes in to talk and I show them one of these babies. They have the same observation you have." Said Bill. "It works great, but this baby has more than a good wax job. Come check this out."

The three men climbed the steps of a moveable stairway up to the door of the aircraft and into the passenger area. Josh made himself comfortable in one of the seats while Bill and Pete walked forward and through the open door and into the cockpit, seating themselves in the pilot and co-pilot seats.

"That company you hired did a great job on the insides of this baby. The leather on these seats is so soft. Must have cost a fortune!" said Josh.

"Well, it wasn't cheap", said Bill with a proud smile.

"How about some music guys?" Pete flips a switch somewhere on the cockpit console. Several small green and red console lights display, and the music swells the cabin of the plane.

"Music sounds great. So, how fast will this beauty go?" Josh asked.

"The Citation 10 is the fastest civil aircraft in the world, replied Bill. It has a top end of about 700 miles per hour and a cruising range of 3000 miles before we have to pull into the next *Quik Trip* and gas up," replied Bill.

Bill moved out of the pilot's seat and back toward to where Josh was sitting.

"Let's go back down. I want to show you something else." Said Bill.

The two climbed down the stairs to the hangar floor. Josh followed as Bill stooped and moved under the wing of the plane's belly.

"Okay Pete, let's show Josh where we keep the Saturday Night Special."

Suddenly, two small doors on both sides of the fuselage open. From each of the openings came a whirring sound and with that appeared a high caliber gun, slowly and precisely positioning themselves into place.

"What are you guys planning to do with all this firepower?" asked Josh. "I'm no gun expert, but those guns are what, fifty caliber?"

"Yep, they're pretty cool, aren't they?" Bill replied. "Our customers' needs keep changing so in this highly competitive business, we've got to meet those needs. I know you've heard that before."

"Sure, but what happened to cause you to equip a plane like this?" asked Josh.

"We had a customer not long ago come into my office and asked if we would be able to protect our aircraft in an emergency. He was a young fellow, had kind of a Hollywood hip hop style, so I didn't give it more than a little consideration." Bill explained. "One day, an older gentleman, dressed in banker style, you know—dark suit and tie, came in here and asked the same question. Said he sometimes carries important documents on him. Turns out the younger man was some kind of a software genius. Created one of those mobile phone apps that was off the chain!"

Bill started laughing so hard he started to choke. Pete throws him a bottle of water from the open cockpit door. Bill took a sip.

"He was able to pay the price, but we couldn't deliver. Now we can. I figure in the world we live in, I had better listen to my customers and protect them and my business from pirating, kidnapping and all the rest of that crap." Bill took a drink of the bottled water. "I'm going to call both of those guys back and let them know I can deliver what they need."

Josh hears his cell phone.

"Just a minute guys, I gotta' take this call. It's from Sharon."

"Okay, tell her hello for me. I haven't seen her in forever!" said Bill.

"Hey Sharon."

Josh, I'm on my way to pick up Savannah from school. I've had a busy day."

"Oh yeah?" David got you guys hopping today?"

"Well, we have a big deal working. I may be spending some time in the Caymans."

"Sounds, like a great assignment," said Josh. "Never been to the Cayman Islands."

"I know, I'll tell you more about it later."

"Okay, so what else is going on today?" Josh quizzed.

"A man called me. Says his name is Warren James. He's called me several times, but I kept putting him off. Well, we finally connected, and he wants to talk about the crash."

"Talk about the crash?" Josh said suspiciously. Who is this Warren James? What does he know about the crash or anything else about us?"

"I have the same thoughts about it as you Josh, but he was really interested about meeting privately to discuss anything more. He seemed to know a lot about you and the investigation business." Sharon said. "I guess he's done some homework."

"Well, what do you want to do?" Josh asked.

"I was thinking it might be worth at least one meeting to see where this takes us. He says he knows we are privately working on the details of Ali's crash. If he is solid on this maybe we should let him help us."

Josh was quiet for a moment.

"You still there Josh?"

"Oh, sorry. I was just thinking about Ali. Okay, give him a call back and set something up. We'll see where it goes."

"Sounds good, I'll let you know. Gotta' go now." Sharon said hurriedly. "Talk to you later."

11

Sharon steers the Porsche into the pickup area of the school. She was a little early. The big clock standing on the front lawn of the school said there was still ten minutes left before school was out. Sharon thought she would relax a little while she waited for Savannah. Shutting down the engine, she sits back in her seat. There was no snow on the ground yet. The grass of the school campus still showed some green in places, the mark of a warmer season, summer, and the promise of its return. Snowflakes, scant and light, drifted toward the ground. It was one of the first really cold winter days. Sharon was starting to get a little cold now, so she started the engine to warm up. Soon she sees Savannah walking across the campus with several of her classmates. She could hear the voices laughing and joking as they walked toward the car.

"See you tomorrow!" Savannah yells as the others headed for the other cars waiting for them. She opens the car door of the black Porsche and hops in, throwing her backpack behind the seat.

"Hey Mom, you been waiting long?!"

"I got here a little early, but not too long. Have a good day?"

"Okay, I guess." Savannah said softly, pausing, gazing through the windshield into somewhere.

"When are you leaving for those islands?" said Savannah, refocusing.

"Not sure yet, I still have some research stuff to do before I take off."

"Wish I could go with you."

"Well, that's a possibility. Rene's folks live in the Cayman Islands. Maybe we all might get a chance to go."

"Hey, that would be great!" Savannah was excited.

"Maybe we can go at spring break, depending on how things work out. So, what are your plans for tonight, after homework of course?"

"No homework tonight Mom. I got a great idea, though."

"Oh, what is your great idea?"

"Let's go shopping, I need a new swimsuit to take to the Caymans!"

"Hey, aren't you jumping the gun a bit?" Sharon said smiling. "I don't have a travel date yet."

"Oh, c'mon Momma, I can still wear it when summer comes, even if we don't go!"

Sharon found it hard to resist Savannah's request. She figured losing Ali, her sister and only sibling, had stolen that short period of childhood and innocence. Sharon was going to do her best to make it right for her, no matter what.

12

Josh sits in his leather recliner watching the television screen watch him. It's been a busy day and he decides to just take it easy for the evening. Surfing through several channels he decides to work on his scrapbook of family photos and clippings he acquired going back almost three centuries of family history. Leafing through the pages of the old scrapbook always brought comfort, especially now. He can still remember his grandfather's voice. *"Run Josh, run!"* Josh could hear his grandfather's voice in the background as he ran in the pasture on the old Louisiana farm. He was running, free as the wind. He stepped up the pace, he felt good. His strong heart and body and a youth pair of legs. He ran like a gazelle. He heard his grandfather's voice again. Run Josh!" This time the tone was different. There was a sense of urgency and fear, something he had not heard before. Josh jerked himself up in his chair. A bead of sweat rolled down his neck as he laid the old scrapbook on the lamp table next to him. Josh realized he had fallen asleep, if only for a moment. He thought about his grandfather and decided to go on to bed. He turned off the lamp next to the recliner and made his way to the bedroom. Josh turned on the television, slips on his pajamas and slides into bed. He thought again about his grandfather's voice in that short dream as he plumped up his pillow. *Just a wide-awake dream,* he thinks to himself.

Josh awakes the next morning a little earlier than usual. His cell phone tells him it is not yet six o'clock in the morning, but it's close enough. Sitting up in the bed, he checks his cell phone for his appointments for the day. First it would be the gym as usual and then a phone call to Sharon to see what she learned from that meeting with that Warren James fellow. Christmas was only a few days away now. It hadn't snowed yet. The morning sky was overcast, and it had that grey, cloudy look that warned it might snow like the dickens any moment now. Josh gets out of bed walked across the bedroom and opened the closet door. Josh grabs a freshly laundered shirt and a starched pair of Wrangler jeans. He pulls on a pair of Luchese boots and walks to the kitchen. There he places a K-Cup into the machine and a coffee cup under the dispenser. He walked to the front door of the condo. He walked outside and picked up the morning Kansas City Star newspaper from the driveway. The air was cold and slightly damp, perfect weather for the first snowfall of the season. Josh remembered his plan to call Sharon. He punched the numbers into his cell phone and waits for the ring. Sharon didn't answer, and the call goes to voicemail. Josh generally didn't leave Sharon voicemail messages. He knew she would return his call when she saw the missed call from him. But this time he did just in case he got busy later and wouldn't be able to answer. He was anxious to meet this man who seemed to know about Josh, but Josh knew little about him. This made him anxious about the meeting. Josh backed the Buick out of the garage and heads toward the gym. He meets Bill in the locker room. The two friends share the same daily workout routine.

"Hey Josh, good mornin'!" Bill always seemed to be his best in the morning.

"Hey Bill, what's up with you today? You look locked and loaded as usual!" Josh smiles as the two bump fists.

I'm great, ready to go this morning! How about you?" said Bill.

"I'm working on something. I need to follow up on some information I learned from the highway patrolman who chased the truck. He did the initial reports."

"Hmm, that's interesting," said Bill grabbing a towel from the rack. "He gave you a copy of those reports?"

"Not exactly, but we talked privately. Sharon told me she got a call from some guy claiming to have some information. He wants to meet up."

"Well, my friend, if I can help in anyway, you can depend on me."

13

Lace Benton was sitting in the chair behind Josh's desk when he walked into the office of JL Investigations. Josh wasn't surprised see
her, but he wasn't expecting a visit either. She wore a pair of brown English riding boots and beige riding pants that clung to her still youthful figure. A reminder to the observer that she was still viable in her forties. She was smart and tough.

"So, where you been detective?" Lace said with a wink.

Josh pretended to be unmoved by this comment from his unexpected guest. He walked over to the pile of mail sitting on the corner of his desk and pretended to sort through it as if he was looking for something important, which he wasn't.

"Hi Lace, I wasn't expecting a visit from you so early in the morning. Besides, I haven't seen or heard from you in what, a month or so?'

"Absence makes the heart grow fonder", she said smiling slyly. "I hope you don't mind if I use a tired old cliché'?

Josh continued to look through the mail, throwing the junk in an old wooden waste basket setting on the floor next to his desk.

"Aren't you glad to see your old high school girlfriend? You can't pretend we don't still have that thing."

She took her legs off the desk, stood up and came straight to Josh, touching her nose to his.

Josh tried to step back, then moved to the other side of the desk, but Lace kept the pressure on. The chemistry remained, but they agreed long ago it wouldn't work in a steady relationship. Josh was too steady; she was too restless.

Lace pushed Josh down onto the chair and she sat on the side of the desk facing him.

"Seriously Josh, I really would like to help you with something. You can use my help, can't you? I heard you were still trying to pin down something about the crash, right?" said Lace, voice almost pleading. "I want to do something for Ali. I remember her too."

The expression on her face was real and Josh couldn't reject her.

"Well, I might need your help later, but not just yet. You need to make sure I can catch up with you when I need you."

"That's not a problem, I still have the same cell number I've had forever. If you called sometimes, you'd know that."

Josh looked at her, squinting his eyes in response.

"Oh, I forgot about Sharon." Lace said coyly. "You guys still together, I guess?"

"We're still together."

"That's okay." She said with a smile. "I like a challenge."

"You always did like to go for whatever was sort of out of your reach," said Josh.

"So, what's wrong with that may I ask? All I said was I like a challenge," Lace said.

"Well, nothing, I guess. You always seem to be looking for another place to hoist your flag. But that's all good! Anyway, enough of the small talk. I've got to make a couple of phone calls about the crash. Make yourself comfortable if you like."

"That would be nice if I had the time." Lace said glancing her watch. "Right now, I have to get going, but if you need my help later, just give me a call."

"Hold up a minute, there is one thing you can do for me when you can."

"What's that?"

"Find out everything you can about the truck company the driver worked for and anything else involved, weight, cargo, shipping details…whatever, as soon as you can."

"I'll get back to you as soon as I have something." Lace said smiling. She turned walked out the office door, gently closing it behind her.

14

Warren James sits drinking coffee in the cafeteria of the Teamsters Truckers Union. It is 6:30 in the morning and except for a few food service workers, he is the only office employee in the building. Warren still liked to read the morning paper before getting things going and thought it was important to be there early whenever he could.

No news today, he thinks to himself. *I might as well look at all the Christmas ads and go shopping!* He enjoyed this quiet time of the morning. This is my home, isn't *it? Well almost, it wouldn't be healthy, if I liked this place that much!* he chuckled to himself.

He gets up from the table and walks toward the counter to get a refill. Then, having second thoughts, he turns around and sits the half empty cup of coffee on the table.

"Morning Warren, cutting down on the caffeine?"

"Hey, how you doing George? Nah, you know they never make good coffee around here."

"Warren, I think you done let them high falootin' preppy fellows at them coffee shops you been going to get too close to you." George said laughing.

"Maybe, but I think it's time we need to step it up a bit. Who says truckers can't drink good coffee?"

Warren James looked up from the counter at George. George looked back at him through a pair of squinting eyes and a tan, leathered face. He always had a quizzical look on his face, as if he were about to ask you an important question, or he was waiting for an answer of some sort.

"So, George, what's happening on your side of the house?" Warren asked. "Equipment in good shape?" Warren James already knows the equipment was probably in excellent shape. George's team of mechanics and technicians always kept things in great shape.

"Always something to fix, but overall we are ready to go 24-7. Keeping the trucks up and running I can do. It's those damn safety regulations that worry me." George said, showing some frustration. "I have to educate *and* motivate my drivers. They just want to drive their load to its destination and get paid!"

"I know George, I know. We all have our jobs to do. In the meantime, make sure those GPS recorders are installed and working. I'll go to all those damn government watchdog meetings!"

Warren James didn't like this part of his job. It wasn't much fun hassling with all those public safety regulations.

"Hell, Jim. You know I'll get the job done. I mean, we'll get the job done! Get it done like we always have, you and me!"

George was back to himself again. That squint in his eyes and the same smile Warren James had known for years. Years that carried them both back to when they drove those big rigs, barely getting enough sleep, driving too many miles to earn enough to feed their families.

"Time to get to my office and start the day. We've got to go for a beer like we used to."

"You mean like before, when we weren't so important?" said George smiling.

"Yeah, like before."

Warren James patted George on the shoulder, turned and walked out of the cafeteria and down the spit-shined tile floor which led into a carpeted main lobby. Libby, the lead receptionist looked up briefly as Warren passed her desk, She raised her hand, acknowledging his presence. Warren James could see she was already busy with incoming calls, so he raised his hand, smiled and just kept walking. The carpet continued down another hallway and opened into the executive office of the company. Warren James walked into his office and sat down in one of the guest chairs facing his desk. Something he had a habit of doing. Often, he would sit there reading his mail or a report when a coworker would walk in to discuss a project. He would have them take a seat in the big leather chair at his desk. He had no hang-ups regarding position or power as expressed through inanimate objects, so long as that power and control stayed with him.

"Mr. James, there is an officer John Speight on your line." It was Libby.

"Okay, Libby, ask him to hold for a few moments if he can."

"I'll tell him. He's on line one."

Warren James walked to the back of his office and reached for a file sitting on the corner of his desk. The file was simply labeled *Missouri 70*. He picks up the desk phone and presses the button under the flashing light."

"Good Morning, this is Warren James. What can I do for you Officer Speight?"

"Morning Mr. James, it's been a while, I know. I thought I might take few minutes of your time to follow up on the Landrieu case. I apologize for the time it has taken since we last talked."

"I understand Officer Speight, I've got a few years of experience on this stuff, so I know it takes time to sort out. So, what do we talk about today?"

Well, Mr. James, we've been running background checks on the driver of the tractor trailer. We found what we call a rabbit hole and we haven't been able to come out of it. Questions have come up. Questions we think you can help us with."

"Okay, what would you like to know?" Warren James was always cooperative with law enforcement. It made his job easier.

"Well, we verified he was a union driver for the last seven years. We also know prior to that he was in transportation as a driver, a warehouse laborer and an equipment operator in heavy construction. This is probably stuff you already know."

"Probably, but that's okay." Replied Warren James. "Go on please."

What we do know is that the merchandise he was hauling that day doesn't belong to the company listed on the manifest. We are still checking out information on the company which appears to be located somewhere in the Caribbean."

"What's the name of the company?

"Just a minute, let me look."

There was a pause in the conversation. Warren James could hear Officer Speight rustling through a paper file.

"Just a minute, let me look. It looks like a code name or something. Ah, here it is. Looks like Daimler 8 or something. Does that sound like a name you recognize Mr. James?"

"It isn't ringing any bells, but I can check it out and let you know if I find anything close to that name."

"That would be helpful. Please give me or the department a call if you do. We will be in touch if there is anything further. Have a good day."

Warren James hung up the phone. He didn't like the sound of any of this.

15

"Hey Mom, I think this one looks cute on me! What do you think?" Samantha spun around and modeled the new swimsuit. Sharon flashed back on an earlier time, when she, Samantha and Ali went shopping together. The memory was both joy and pain. But she was enjoying this time with Savannah. It helped her push through it.

"I think it looks great on you. How does it feel? It isn't too tight is it? I think you're a little taller than last year, so make sure it feels right. What about the other one? Maybe you should try it on again.

"Nah, I think I like this one. It feels right. Can I get this one Momma?"

"Sure, but we better get some dinner soon, it's getting late and I'm a little tired."

"Me too", said Savannah. "Let's just get some carryout and watch some TV at home."

The two gathered up their things and walked quickly through the store, passing the colorful Christmas displays and salespeople offering perfume and cologne samples. It was dark when Sharon and Savannah pulled into the driveway and opened the garage door. They got out of the Porsche. The garage door closed as the two grab their bags and walk up the three wooden steps leading from the garage and through the door leading into the kitchen. Samantha throws her coat on a kitchen chair and gets paper plates from the pantry.

"Savannah, could you warm up the pizza a little please? I'm going to get rid of these heels and find my old jeans."

"I'm way ahead of you momma, hurry up in there, I'm hungry."

"You go ahead and eat, don't wait for me!" Sharon yelled from the bedroom.

Sharon walks into the kitchen and sits down at the table. She grabs a slice of pizza, quickly tossing it on a paper plate.

"Ouch, that's hot!"

"Well, you told me to warm it up!" Samantha laughed.

"I know, guess I'm really hungry!"

The two eat the pizza together, enjoying the moment. Sharon turns on the television suspended from the ceiling just above the sink Savannah flips through a magazine.

"So, what's going on at school?" Sharon asks.

"Oh, just everybody talking about what they are going to do for Christmas vacation. I'm thinking about trying out for the tennis team when spring comes. There was something about tryouts on a bulletin board in one of my classrooms."

"Hey, that's great. Guess that means we have to get you a couple of cute tennis outfits too, right?" Sharon was smiling.

"I think we have a team outfit, Momma, but still a good idea!" Samantha said, giving her Mom a thumbs up.

"Your grades going to be good for this semester?"

"Of course, Momma, you've seen all the grades this year and you ask me that every week, nearly every day."

"And you are studying for those semester exams, right? You can always blow it at the end."

Savannah rolls her eyes.

"Never mind, I just worry about you all the time. That's what…"

"I know, that's what mothers do," Savannah echoes.

They both laugh and smile. There was silence for a moment. The two, mother and daughter look at the empty chairs at the table. They miss the four of them eating pizza together. The Christmas season is bittersweet. They miss Ali.

"Well, I have to get ready to go to the office in the morning."

"You do?" Savannah asked.

"Well, yeah. Right now, you're the only one on Christmas vacation around here! It's Friday, so if nothing important happens today, we can start the weekend. How about that?"

"Okay, sounds good Momma."

16

"Sharon quietly peeks through the slightly opened door of Savannah's bedroom. She sees Savannah still in slumber, so she slipped quietly down the hall and through the kitchen. The pizza box with three pieces lay open on the kitchen counter along with the paper plate and plastic cups from a few hours before. Sharon backed the Porsche out of the garage and headed onto the street. The sun's light cuts through the snowy gray sky of the morning. It's rays glinting off the light frost covering the landscape. The naked beauty of the Winter Solstice. Traffic is light. Everyone is home preparing for The Great Day. *Except for us Warriors.* Sharon joked to herself. She parked the car and sprinted across the parking lot covered with the morning frost. *Glad I wore my sneaker today, slippery out here!*

The office building is quiet. Just a few people in the complex putting the final touches on their work before the celebrations begin. Sharon gets off the elevator and walked across the lobby and into the offices of Cavanaugh International.

"I thought I was going to be the only here today." Rene said with a smirk.

"Hey Rene! Well, I'm planning to get in and out if we don't have any surprises. Savannah is out of school for the holidays and I want to spend this weekend with her. She's going to be with Josh for the New Year weekend. Rene, I need you to plan a trip to the

Caymans for me shortly after the New Year. Say, around mid-January. The world will get back to business as usual by then.

"I'm on it. What about David?"

"Not sure what his plans are yet, but it will probably be shortly after that. Maybe about a week or so."

Sharon walked into her office, taking off her wool knit cap and scarf. She throws them along with her white parka onto the little sofa facing her desk. She sorts through the various letters and correspondence and picks up the note scribbled a few days earlier reminding her of the call with Warren James. She paused a moment, staring at the little yellow Post It note. She picked up the phone and dialed the number.

No way he's going to be there. It's too close to Christmas.

"Hello."

Oh, Hello, this is Sharon Landry." Sharon replied, surprised to hear the voice. "Is this Warren James?"

"Yes, it is. Good morning Mrs. Landry. I am surprised and pleased to hear from you. I wasn't expecting to discuss to hear from you so close to the Holidays."

"Well, Mr. James, I wasn't expecting you to answer when I called, for the same reason."

"Possibly we are starting out on a good note, seems we seem to think alike. You and I, working while everyone else is enjoying themselves.

"A bit early to assume similarities Mr. James, don't you think? But I do appreciate the compliment." Sharon hates it when men try to mix a little flattery into a business discussion with a woman. She's still uneasy with that voice.

"Anyway, I ran across my reminder to call you to further discuss information you claim to have." Sharon said.

"I would rather refer to it as information sharing. A discussion we can both benefit from. Would it be acceptable to you to schedule a meeting shortly after the New Year?"

"Okay, I think I can be available the first week in January," Sharon said, glancing at the calendar on her phone."

"How about on the third of January?"

"Fine, at six o'clock at that bar at the Union Station. The one right in the middle of the lobby near the entrance." Sharon replied.

"Thank you, Mrs. Landry, I will see you then. Have a nice holiday season and Merry Christmas.

"You as well Mr. James, goodbye."

Sharon ends the call. Rene walks in and sits on the little sofa next to the desk.

"Sharon, here are some flight dates for you to look at, different times, different days, airlines, etcetera."

Rene hands Sharon a schedule of airlines departing Kansas City in January. You can tell me which one you would like me to book and I'll get going on it."

Sharon studies the information for a few moments.

"I think the January 10th date will work. Thanks Rene."
Sharon gives the sheet of information back to Rene.

"Rene, is David in today?"

"I haven't seen him. Have you tried his office?"

"No, I don't expect him in today. Just thought I'd ask. In that case, I'm going to finish up and get out of here before something keeps me from it!" Sharon says.

"I'm right behind you!" said Rene, nodding her head in agreement.

17

Josh sat in his office glaring at the Apple computer when Bill Haus lit up the caller ID on Josh's phone. He slides the answer button.

"Hey Bill, what's up?"

"Nothing much, just the usual stuff in the airplane leasing business!" Bill always gave you the impression he was always in good spirits, even if he wasn't.

I've missed you at the gym the last couple of days. Thought I would check in on you, my friend."

"Yeah, I know. Sorry about that Bill. It's starting to get a little busy around here. Wasn't expecting it, this time of the year.

Well, it's great to hear you still kicking! Any new developments on the crash? I know you been working on that. The police or anybody figured out any more about what happened?"

"Not yet, but I was just getting ready to call the officer who wrote the report."

"You mean that officer Speight guy? I remember you mentioning him some time ago."

"Yeah, that's him," Josh replied. "I haven't heard from him lately."

"Hey, buddy I got a call coming in. I'll call you later."

"Okay, talk later." Josh said.

Josh looks for Officer Speight's number."

"John Speight."

"Hello, Officer Speight. This is Josh Landry."

"Mr. Landry, how are you? I have been meaning to call you."

"We haven't talked in a while, so I thought I would check in."

"That's fine, I'd glad you did. Our truck driver has disappeared."

"You mean he has skipped bail!?" Josh felt his heart pick up the beat. "Well, where is he?"

"We don't know yet. We have our detectives on the search."

"You need my help."

"Mr. Landry, we would love to have your experience and we understand the personal concern here, but I have to professionally tell you---"

"I know the routine. You won't even know I've been there. Is there anything else?" Josh asked briskly."

"That's pretty much it for right now."

"Thanks for giving me the update." Said Josh.

"You're welcome. Oh, Mr. Landry, just between two cops, if you do find something or find the trucker, please let me know. I'll do the same." The call went dead.

Josh sat in the chair for a moment, his thought reviewing the conversation with the policeman. He picks up the phone and calls Bill.

"Calling back so soon, my friend? I didn't figure we'd talk so soon! Something must be up, right?"

"Right, I just got off the phone with Speight. He says somehow they lost track of the trucker."

"You mean he jumped bail," said Bill flatly, "well, what do you want to do?"

"I'm not sure yet. I'm still thinking about it."

"Did Speight have any clues as to where he might be?"

"He didn't say exactly, but I'm not waiting on them. Can you get away for a drink later?" asked Josh.

"Sure, where do you want to go?"

"How about that quiet little place near the old stockyards, say about six o'clock?"

"See you at six."

Josh looked at the time on the computer screen. It was almost four o'clock in the afternoon. He glanced across the room at the file lying on a window ledge in the corner of the office. He had almost forgotten about it. An elderly man had come to him a few weeks before Ali's death asking Josh to help him find a daughter he had lost contact with some time ago. A daughter born of a passionate romance when he was a younger man. Josh didn't have the time now to find her. He decided he would ask Lace to do it.

18

The drive into downtown Kansas City at the end of the day is a little easier than driving out of it, but busy none the less. The Buick heads west, crawling through the tight interchanges and crowded overpasses that eventually dump into the old stockyards at the Missouri-Kansas border. Josh pulls into the parking lot of the old steakhouse. Bill arrived ahead of him. Josh recognizes the black Escalade. On its tailgate is the emblazoned image of a Falcon, its talons extended ready to catch its prey. Bill is still sitting in the SUV as Josh pulls into the parking space next to him. Bill waves and gets out. He talks to someone on his cell phone as they walk across the parking lot through the glass door and into the restaurant.

"A table for two please." Josh says to the host as the two men walk in. "We don't have a reservation."

"That's okay, we have a table for you." He replies. "Just follow me, please.

Bill and Josh followed the host toward a booth on the left wall of the restaurant. The two men sit opposite each other while the servers bring water and menus. Bill ends his conversation and places the cell phone on the table.

"Sorry about that, taking care of business. So, what's for dinner? Bill says picking up the menu.

"I think I'm going to order a cocktail first, but I'm going to have the ribeye. Steak is what they do best here." Said Josh

"I'm going to follow your lead on that." Bill motioned the waiter to the table.

"Good evening, what can I get for you?" The waiter asks.

"I'd like to have a Manhattan please. Make it a good one."

"I'll have a Martini and don't forget the olives." Says Josh.

The waiter nodded and turned toward the bar.

"Wow, man that's some crazy news," says Bill. "So, what's the plan Josh? I know you are going to try to find this guy, so how can I help?"

"I think we should start with this guy who called Sharon a few days ago. He says he has something we need to know. Sharon says she plans to meet with him soon. I'm going to wait to see what comes out of that."

"So, what's the connection with this person?" asks Bill.

"All I know right now is that he is in the trucking business. Not sure in what capacity, but if he is bold enough to call Sharon, then there must be something there, don't you think?"

"I would think so. Maybe you should pay a visit to this...what's his name?"

"James, Warren James, I think that's his name. Yeah, I thought about that. In fact, I might do just that," Josh pauses, "after Sharon talks to him."

"Yeah, probably a good idea." Bill says laughing.

"So, how are you and Jessie these days? You still making her feel like a queen?" Josh said smiling.

"We're going great." Bill replies. "We need to get the girls together sometime. It would be like old times!"

"Let's do that next time we have dinner together. Here come our drinks. Let's order those steaks!

Josh and Bill pass the next two hours enjoying the time together about their days of ending youth. The time when adolescence begins its task with the pimpled scarring of young boys faces. The first change away from being boys and the beginning of the *Journey of Men*. Days when baseball and sharing a Playboy magazine stolen from an uncle or older brother, or just hanging out was the order of the day. Days before girls came into the discussion, before the high school prom and varsity letter jackets. Before the first kiss, the first love. Hell, *before the first time*, way before that for most. Days just before getting a driver's license. The two men order another cocktail and toast those gone days. Those days before loss.

"Let's go find that son a bitch." Says Bill.

Aside from the cocktails, the drive home was easy. Josh steered the Buick out of the West Bottoms and headed south to the suburbs. He took a main street through the city, avoiding the interstate. He liked to drive the boulevards. Tonight, is a good night for that. The night before Christmas Eve the houses along the boulevards sparkle with the lights of the Season. Some were unique, others not so much, but it added to the drive through the Country Club Plaza and on south of the city. Josh switches the radio to a satellite station. He hears Johnny Mathis singing *When a Child is*

Born. A full moon casts a Broadway glow on the city, illuminating the landscape and the road as Josh heads home. Tomorrow he would spend the evening and Christmas Day with Sharon and Samantha. They would spend it alone this time. Just them, no other family and the accompanying stress of the Holidays to distract them from the bonding and remembrance of what it is all supposed to be about.

Josh pushes the garage door remote and pulls in next to the Camaro. He is home. His cell phone lights up before he could get out of the car, it was Lace Benton.

"Hey Lace, you don't usually call this late. You find out something about that Daimler 8 thing?"

"No, but I'm working on it. I was just getting ready to get some sleep. I thought about our little talk today and thought I'd check in and see how the rest of your day went."

"Well, I talked to Bill shortly after you left the office and we met for a couple of drinks and dinner."

"Boys' night out?" Lace said, laughter in her voice.

"Seriously though Josh, I really want to help you on your investigation."

"I'm serious too, get me some stuff on that Daimler thing, everything is important. There's one more thing."

"What's that?"

I could really use your help locating an old man's daughter. He's lost track of her and its important he reconnect with her soon."

"Sure, I'll help you on that."

"Okay, thanks Lace. I'll email you the info tomorrow and you can get started."

Josh realizes he was still sitting in his car.

"Talk to you later and Merry Christmas."

"Merry Christmas, Josh, nite'."

19

Christmas Eve morning Josh is at the computer pulling up the file of the old man trying to find his lost child. He skimmed the info. Her name is Christina Capelli. She is 60 years old, a few years older than Josh. She has one child, her husband a career Marine officer. Last residence was in northern California. Josh attached the file and sent it on to Lace. After that he had coffee and dressed to do what everybody does on this day.

Okay, time to tackle the Christmas shopping. Josh said to himself. He spends the next few hours at the shopping malls around the city, looking for a gift for Sharon and Savannah.

It was midafternoon when Josh finished his day with the purchase of a pretty birthday anniversary bracelet for Sharon. It had the birthstones of Ali and Savannah, something he knew Sharon would like. Josh looks at his watch. It was almost four o'clock. He decides to call Sharon.

"I was just about to call, you beat me to it." Sharon laughs.

"I've been busy with stuff. What are you and Savannah doing, are you home yet?"

"We're just about to head for the house. We've got one more stop to make and then we we're on our way."

"Okay, see you soon." Said Josh.

Josh was in the kitchen preparing some snacks for the three of them when his cell phone signaled a new text message from Sharon.

On our way now, want me to pick up anything?

Josh thought for a moment and texts back.

Maybe soda or something for Sam. I don't have any.

Josh looked up at the television suspended in the corner of the kitchen as he picked up the knife and began peeling shrimp for the gumbo he was preparing for dinner. He could see the news banner scrolling across the bottom of the screen.

Cayman Islands Prime Minister to announce new transportation and trade policy.

Josh couldn't hear the broadcast. Sometimes he liked to play music in the background while the television was muted, particularly when he was preparing a meal or just reading the newspaper.

He heard the doorbell ring and the sound of the front door opening. Josh could see the black Porsche parked in the driveway from the kitchen window.

"Come on in, it's open!" he shouted.

"Hey Dad, what ya' doin?!" Savannah said, walking briskly into the kitchen. She took off her coat and scarf and hugged Josh, giving him a quick kiss on the cheek."

"Hey Savannah, where's your Mom?" Josh asked.

"Not far behind." Sharon said from the hallway. "What are you cooking? Smells good."

"Doing my best to cook grandma's good ole' Louisiana gumbo." Josh looked up at them with a proud smile. "My grandpa used to say, that is one beautiful, mean woman…"

"…but she sure can cook!" Sharon and Savannah joined in with Josh and broke into laughter. They had heard Josh remember his grandparents in this way many times before.

"I still have to cook some rice for the gumbo, but that won't take very long. I made a cheese tray and crackers and I sliced some summer sausage to snack in the meantime."

Sharon mixed the cornbread batter, while Savannah sat at the counter eating cheese and crackers and drinking some punch Sharon made.

"This time last year it was four of us." Said Samantha, breaking the silence. "I miss my sister."

"There will always be the four of us." Said Josh, embracing Savannah and Sharon. "We all miss Ali."

They stood in the kitchen, hugging each other. Then the doorbell rang.

"Wonder who that could be." Said Josh.

He walked out of the kitchen to the front door and peeps through the spy hole, but he doesn't see anybody. He opens the door to find Bill and Jamie. They were stooped below the spy hole, so Josh couldn't see them.

"Surprise!" They both yell.

"You guys are crazy, come on in!" Josh said.

Sharon and Samantha come out to the hallway to see what's going on.

"Oh my god, it's been so long since I've seen you two!" Sharon said. "Come on in, let me take your coats."

"You're just in time to have Gumbo with us." Said Josh.

"Well, we brought some champagne! Said Jamie."

"Great, I'll get some glasses. We'll have a toast." Said Sharon.

Sharon sat the glasses on the table and poured the champagne. Bill raises his glass for the toast.

"Here's to our very good friends, our family as we celebrate. But most of all, here's to Ali."

They enjoy the evening and the meal and chatting about time gone by. The fun and the time go by quickly. Jamie yawns and nods at Bill.

"I guess we need to get home to bed." Said Bill looking at his watch. "It's almost midnight."

"Yeah, I'm getting a little tired too. Thanks for coming over. What a great evening." Said Josh.

Samantha had fallen asleep on the living room sofa.

"Think I'll go to bed," Sharon yawns. "we can clean up the kitchen tomorrow."

Samantha sat up and stretched. "I'm going to bed too."

Josh had just fallen asleep when he heard a gentle chime. He thought it was a dream he was having that woke him up. The half-conscious kind we all have from time to time. The music continued. Josh sat up in the bed.

"Sharon, do you hear that?"

"I think so, sounds like a wind chime or something."

Josh got out up and walked down the hallway past Savannah's room to the living room. There he could hear a little music box playing *Silent Night.* Josh thought it strange it was playing all on its own. He couldn't remember the last time it even played. He turned and walked back toward the bedroom. He paused when he saw Savannah sitting up in her bed.

It's okay Dad, it's Ali. She's letting us know she is with us tonight."

20

Warren James sits in his office looking out at the last sunset he would see in December. The office was quiet, peaceful. Not unusual for New Year's Eve, most of the employees were already on vacation. He glanced at his watch. It was already 4:30. He and his wife Marie are expecting guests for the evening. He picked up the phone to call just in case Marie might want him to pick up something on the way home. She answers the phone on the first ring.

"Hi, you on your way home, I hope."

"Just about to walk out the door as we speak."

"Good, sweetheart would you stop on your way and pick up some club soda and tonic water for cocktails? We're short on club soda and the tonic has gone flat."

"Okay, I can do that."

Warren James see another call coming in on the phone, flashing Officer Speight.

"I'll be home in about thirty minutes, honey, bye."

He swaps the call over to connect his caller.

"Hello, Officer Speight," said Warren James.

"Mr. James, I wasn't expecting you to answer the phone this evening. I was planning to leave a voicemail message."

"Another five minutes and you would have missed me. How can I help?"

"Just one question. I was wondering if you might have any information regarding the Daimler truck thing?

Warren paused a moment, wondering how he should respond to that question.

"Nothing more than we've already discussed." Warren said shortly. "Something else come up I should know about?"

"Well, I'm not at liberty to say right now. Trying to verify all information right now. Enjoy your evening Mr. James."

"You as well Officer Speight, goodbye."

Warren James looked out the window of his office. It's dark now, the sun's rays snuffed out by the blue indigo of winter.

I better get going. I'm going to be an hour getting home now.

Nearly an hour later, Warren James is home. Stepping from the shower he slipped on the oversized terry cloth robe he brought home a romantic weekend at the Ritz Carlton at Half Moon Bay with Marie. He sees her sitting in front of the large bathroom mirror brushing her hair.

"You work too hard honey. The world will continue with or without you." Marie said.

"I know, this missing trucker thing is bothering me."

"You've been in the business a long time. This is just more of the same stuff isn't it? It goes with the territory." She stands up and kisses him on the cheek." Let's forget about it tonight and enjoy our guests!"

At seven o'clock the first guests arrived and by eight the house was alive with people celebrating the advent of the next several days.

———————————————

21

"Good morning and Happy New Year!"

"Thanks Rene and happy new year to you." Said Sharon.

"Well, here we are back in position. You and Josh and Savannah have a nice time?"

"We did." Sharon walks around Rene's desk, leans over and give Rene a big hug.

"So, what's at the top of the list for the new year?" said Rene.

"Well, I need to get out to the Caymans. That's at the top of my agenda and I need to talk to that Warren James, for starters.

"You want me to get him on the phone for you?" asked Rene.

"Nah, that's okay. I'll do it."

Sharon threw her coat and knit cap on one of the guest chairs and looked for the little post-it-note with James Warren's phone number on it. She calls the number. A familiar voice answers.

"Warren, this is Sharon Landry."

"Good morning Sharon, I'm so glad you called. How can I help you?"

"Warren, I have some time this week to talk as we planned. Are you available?"

"How about this afternoon, say about one o'clock? You pick the spot."

"Okay, the Corner Café in Leawood? Said Sharon.

"Fine, I'll see you then."

She turned to see David standing in the doorway, flashing a warm, pleasant smile. He always smiled when he was with Sharon. She couldn't help but notice.

"Hi David, what's on your mind today?" Sharon said. "As if I can't guess."

"I thought we should catch up a little. We've got to get going on that Cayman trip.

"I think I'll wait until I get an update from You. There's a board of directors meeting coming up in a few days. I need some time to get ready." He paused. "Hey, I know you've been working on helping Josh find the truck driver. I just want you to let me know if I can do anything to help."

"Thanks, that's kind of you. I've got a meeting this afternoon with a trucking big shot. He says he wants to share information."

"Well, good luck." He smiled again and started out the door, bumping into Rene at the same time.

"Excuse me David, I forgot you guys two were still here."

"It's okay Rene, I was just on my way to my office. See you later."

Sharon checked the time on her watch. It was shortly after one o'clock when she walked into the small café. The lunch crowd had started to tail off, so she had no problem finding a small booth in the corner near the windows. She watched the parking lot outside for

Warren James. She was certain she would know him when he came in.

"May I ask if you are Sharon Landry?" the voice came from two tables across the room. Sharon had ignored the man who did not fit the person she expected to see.

"Yes, I'm Sharon."

The well-dressed man in his late fifties, walked over to the booth where Sharon sat. He held a navy-blue sport jacket tossed over his shoulder and wore a well starched white cotton dress shirt and a brightly colored tie that resembled an artist's pallet. He held out his hand.

"I'm Warren James, may I sit down?" Sharon shook his hand.

"Yes, please sit down." Sharon realized that the voice she heard on the phone wasn't as threatening as she had imagined, but his presence in the room was unmistakable.

"Mr. James, you said you had some information for me about the driver of the truck that took my daughter's life." Sharon said.

"Well, let's say I am as interested in finding him as you are, but admittedly for a different reason. Mrs. Landry, I have been in the trucking and shipping business for over twenty years. I have many people depending on me to maintain the integrity of this industry. This man we are both looking for is somewhat of a question mark, a difficulty for me."

"What do you mean when you say he's a difficulty?" Sharon said skeptically.

"I am referring to his employment in our organization. His records are, let's say, incomplete. I think he may be a rogue employee."

"I'm listening." Said Sharon.

Warren James leaned forward in his chair.

"Sometimes we have drivers who manage to get under the organizational radar. They use the company as cover for another illegitimate operation. These people move around from one trucking company to the next, so we don't have a competent means of knowing when they are working inside our network. By the time we discover something unusual, they disappear before we can set up to trap them. Usually at great expense to us.

"You mean they take merchandise in the process."

"Yes. Right now, this discussion stays with us and maybe David Cavanaugh if he chooses to help. In the meantime we both need to focus on an organization called Daimler, or a name similar to that. Right now it's the trail we should be on."

"Any idea where the person might be right now? asked Sharon.

"Not yet, but we're working on it. And if you wish to continue our cooperation, possibly we can get both of our goals accomplished."

Sharon says nothing for a few moments pondering how she should finish the meeting.

"Warren, think we can at least agree to start together on this, but I can't guarantee help from David. He has the say on that." Sharon looked at the old Seth Thomas clock on the far wall. The big hands said it was nearly two o'clock.

"I have to get back to the office. Let's stay in touch. Let me know when you have something more and I'll do the same."

"I can agree to that." Said Warren James.

"They stood up from the café table, grabbing their coats they walk out of the café towards the parking lot, the January wind slapping their faces. Sharon pulls the scarf around her face and walks quickly to the Porsche.

22

The trucker sat alone in the corner of the little café warming his hands on a hot cup of coffee. He watched the townsfolk as they came and went out the cafe door during the evening.

"We'll be closing in about an hour, sir." Would you like to order something before the kitchen closes? Our cook wants to get home for Christmas Eve."

The trucker looks up from his cup of coffee. He sees a woman in her late fifties with long coal black hair pulled back and draped over her left shoulder. He studies her a moment. An attractive woman, he was inclined to make a pass, but decides she probably owned the place with her husband, who was probably the cook. He picked up the menu.

"Is the homemade apple pie as good as this menu says?" The trucker asked.

"It's really good and so is our pecan pie."

"Think I'll have the pecan pie then. Pecan is my favorite." He said in a soft voice, gently touching her forearm. He couldn't hold back any longer. She moved away from his touch.

"That's a good choice, I'll get it for you," she said.

"Bring it to go, please. The cook can get home to his family."

"He's my husband," she replied, feeling the need to make that clear.

The trucker chuckled and thought to himself, *I called it right. I still got the touch.*

The waitress brought out the pie in a white carryout box. She sat the box on the table in front of the trucker.

"Would you like a bag for that?" she said. She placed the bag on the table.

The trucker put the box in the bag, pulled a ten-dollar bill from his wallet and stood up to put on a brown leather flight jacket.

"Thanks, I enjoyed meeting you." He drops the money on the table and walks toward the door. The waitress watches him curiously. She guessed him not to be from New Hampshire, or anywhere else in New England.

"There's a bed and breakfast down the street if you need a place to stay," she said. "and there's a Motel 6 out on the highway, everything else is old or further outside of town."

Ok, thanks…. what's your name anyway?"

"It's Karen."

"Merry Christmas Karen, goodnight."

With that he opened the wood framed door and walked out into the chilly night air. The door slowly closed behind him.

She thought it rude he didn't tell her his name before he left. He watched the man as he climbed up into a white Chevy cargo van and drive away.

23

Josh threw the gym towel into the dirty towel basket. His workout was over. He thought about his plans for the day. He hadn't heard from Lace. Maybe it was time to check in on her as see how she was coming with locating the old man's daughter. His cell phone beeped. It was a text message from Sharon.

Call me when you get a chance

Josh finished dressing, closed the locker door, picked up his workout bag and grabbed his cell phone.

"Hey, I got your text. What's up?"

"I had that meeting yesterday."

"what meeting, you mean that meeting with the trucking guy?

"Yes, that meeting."

"So, did he have anything to say?"

"Let's say it was an interesting conversation. He wants to find this man too. He wants to work with us, you, on it."

"Well, I think he is somewhere in New England. Some little town in New Hampshire or Massachusetts I think." Said Josh.

"Mr. James didn't mention that he knew about that. Maybe he doesn't know that yet." Sharon paused. "Or maybe he's holding back."

"Maybe, we can't assume anything yet. It's too early in the game. We'll worry about that later." Said Josh.

"In the meantime, I'm heading for New England."

"We need to figure out what to do with Savannah, cause I'm going to the Caymans next week." Said Sharon.

"Take her with you, isn't she still on holiday? Jason and Delores would love to see the two of you. Check it out with Rene."

"That's a thought. I did mention it to Savannah. I bought her a new bathing suit just in case."

"Perfect, sounds like a plan to me." Said Josh.

"Okay, call me before you leave town."

"Of course, talk to you later."

Josh saw the black corvette convertible parked next to his parking space as he turned off the Buick's engine. He knew Lace Benton was inside. He hoped she had some good news about the old man, or maybe about the trucker, but he wasn't counting on that. Lace was on the computer talking to someone on Facetime. She held up a finger, acknowledging Josh's presence. Josh could hear a woman's voice. He sat at his desk and sifted through the unopened mail. He texts Bill about his plans to travel to New Hampshire. Bill answers back:

Got business up that way. I can fly us up.

He could smell the perfume Lace was wearing and then he felt her hands gently massage his shoulders. She was standing behind him now.

"I was wondering when you were going to come to work," she smiled. "When you walked in, I was talking to the old man's daughter."

"Really, you found her and she's talking to you Josh said. "Have you told the old man?"

"Yes, I found her and no, I haven't told him yet. But I will, just as soon as I cut through some personal issues," Lace said. "I'm trying to get the two of them together. We're trying to find a good place and time."

"Alright!" Josh said. He walked over to Lace and gave her a high five. She wrapped her arms around his neck and hugged him. The two of them stood there in momentary embrace, thinking of the many years they have been friends, companions and confidants.

"I guess we're soul mates Josh, you and me. So, what's going on with the hunt for the missing trucker?"

"I've got a lead on him up in some little town in New Hampshire. I'm going there tomorrow. Bill is going to fly us up."

"Okay, I'll keep an eye on things here while you are away. I'm going to send an email to Natalie and her father about the arrangements and then I'm headed home."

Josh was surprised Lace hadn't offered to come with him. Lace knew what he was thinking.

"Got a weekend planned with someone," said Lace. She winked at him. "Call me when you and Bill find something."

Josh watches her walk out to the parking lot from the window. She turned and waved. Josh waved back.

24

Josh and Bill could barely see the faint outline of Charlie Wheeler Airport as the Citation quickly gained altitude.

"Where're we going once we get to New Hampshire?" asked Bill.

"To the town of Londonderry. It's closed to Manchester, in the southern part of the state."

"What the heck is he doing in there?" said Bill.

"When a guy is on the run, a *they won't look for me here location* is the first strategy. It's close to Boston and it's a big seaport town."

A smooth ride and three hours later, Bill requests landing instructions.

"ATC Boston Logan, Citation 505KC. We are ten miles west of you; 200 knots, 750 feet, inbound for landing."

"505KC you are cleared for landing on runway 7A"

"Roger, cleared for landing on runway 7A."

Bill drops the landing gear, adjusts the flaps and begins his descent. The plane gently touches down on the runway of Boston Logan International Airport. Two airport personnel in yellow jackets and headphones waved markers as Bill guided the plane toward one of the terminals for private aircraft and shuts down the engines.

"Alright, we made it!" said Josh."

"What, you thought we wouldn't?" Replied Josh grinning.

"Complete confidence. So, what's on your calendar? You said you had business out this way?

"I've got about a half day of business here this afternoon and then I should be free to help you go get the bad guy!"

"Okay, let's go find a room and we can head out to Londonderry tomorrow." Said Josh.

The next morning, they were up early. The two had breakfast at a local breakfast stop close to the airport and then headed up the road for the short drive into town. Josh drove past the townhall and the small 18th century homes mixed with the new architecture of 21st century subdivisions. They saw the Motel 6 and turned into the parking lot. The white delivery truck was still sitting there. Josh got out of the car and walked around the truck.

"See anything?" Bill asked. Josh kept walking around the truck and then stopped.

"I see a travel book of some kind inside the truck." Said Josh. Bill was peering through the window from the other side.

"Looks like he's planning to take a little vacation somewhere in the Caribbean if you ask me."

"Let's check inside with the manager." Said Josh.

The two men walked into the lobby of the motel. A small man wearing a white shirt and a red bow tie sat at the counter behind a glass security window.

"Good morning, can I help you?"

"I'm Josh Landry and this is Bill Haus. We're private investigators. Can you tell me anything about the delivery truck outside?" Josh handed the man a business card. The small man took the card and looked at it.

"Well, I remember checking him in. He didn't talk too much. I can't tell you fellows more than just some general information. You know, privacy laws."

"Did he use a credit card to pay for the room?" asked Josh.

"No, he paid cash. When he took out his wallet, he dropped this card on the counter. He headed straight to his room without picking it up." I guess he didn't see it fall out." The man held the card up to the window. "It's just an old business card for some moving company. A telephone number somewhere in the Caribbean. I was curious, a little nosy maybe, so I checked it out. You can take a look at the room he rented if you like. He paid for one night and left. The police have already been in there. I'll get the key if you like. It's room 103."

"Thanks, we'll take a look." Said Josh.

Josh took the key and walked down the hallway to the room. He slid the plastic card through the reader. A green light flashed, and Josh opened the door. The room was clean and uniform as expected.

"I don't think we are going to find anything here, do you?" said Bill.

"Nah, but we have to stay vigilant. We had to look, and we did. Guess our only lead is the phone number on this card. We can chase it down when we get home."

Bill and Josh close the door and walk back up the hallway to the front lobby. Josh returned the card and the room key to the small man with the red bowtie.

"Thanks for your help." Josh said.

"You're welcome and good luck."

"You ready to head to Nassau?" Bill said, closing the car door. "Let's chase that number down and head on over there!"

"I was thinking of going home first, but maybe we should get a tighter bead on this man might be and go from there. I've got to make some calls first. Let's head back to Manchester and catch a drink somewhere. We can decide what to do and get after it tomorrow."

25

Delores was enjoying her day at the little boutique she had spotted a few days before. It sat near the beach as she had remembered. The shop was nestled in a cluster of small shops reminiscent of earlier days before the factory outlet malls and brand name shops landed on the planet. The shopkeeper smiled as Delores browsed the wares of the store.

"Just make yourself at home dear. Let me know if there is something I can help you with." The woman said, a slight accent. Delores figured it was a mixture of Dutch or German mixed with some long exposure to the islands mixed in. The woman appeared to be in her fifties. Her deep tan and straight brown, sun swept hair disguised any immediate ethnic identification. Delores heard her cell phone signal an incoming call. She reached into her purse, looked at the screen and smiled. It was Rene'.

"Hi sweetheart, how are you this morning!?" Delores was almost giddy.

"Hi mom, I'm doing great, what are you doing?"

"Oh, just doing a little shopping on the beach, enjoying the day. How's the job going? Is Sharon doing okay? Have she and Josh gotten back together yet?" asked Delores.

"No not yet, but I think they are working on it. That's sort of why I'm calling. Sharon is coming there in a few days. She wanted me to let you know." Said Rene.

"That's wonderful. Are you coming with her?"

"Maybe later, I've got to get some support stuff for Sharon and have it ready for her once she gets there, but I might come later. I'll let you know for sure once Sharon arrives. She has a consulting contract there. She says she will call you when she arrives in Grand Cayman."

"That's wonderful. Jason and I will be happy to have some company!" said Delores.

"Okay Mom, I have to go now. Tell Dad hi and I'll call you both later."

"Okay dear, bye."

Savannah helped Sharon pack for her trip. Sharon's mother Madeline would arrive shortly to drive Sharon to the airport. School was back in full swing, so Madeline would stay with Savannah for a few days and then Savannah and Madeline would join Sharon in the

Caymans for a Presidents Day vacation with Jason, Delores and Rene.

A few hours later Sharon was comfortably in her seat as the plane made its way to the east. She hadn't heard from Josh in a couple of days, so she was anxious to hear from him. Sharon wondered when they found the truck driver, would it make any difference in how she felt? *Would it change anything at all?* She thought. She wondered if anything could really find peace and resolution for the loss of Ali. She thought about what Savannah's future would be once she and Josh were gone. Would she find a good husband and have children to spend the rest of her life with, or would it all just simply end in divorce and leave her lonely?

Other people don't have to think about things like this. She thought. *It's not fair.* Sharon sighed as she looked out across the long wing of the aircraft. She ordered a glass of Chardonnay and settled back in her seat for the flight. The hum of the jet engines lulled her to sleep as she stared out the window into the evening sky.

The flight from Kansas City would take 2 stops, one in Charlotte and another in Miami before it arrived in the Caymans. The ding of the seat belt sign woke Sharon from her slumber. The cabin stewards were busy policing the aisles, asking passengers to fasten their seatbelts for the approach into Charlotte. Soon the aircraft was rolling toward the terminal. Sharon didn't have to disembark for the flight to the Caymans. She checked her phone. There was a text message from Josh telling her that he and Bill had made it back to Kansas City. There was also a voicemail message from Warren James. Sharon decides to listen to it later. Soon the sound of landing gear unfolding yielded to the thump of a landing and the plane's engines in reverse thrust, passengers leaning forward in their seats. They were in Miami. She watches as the passengers fetch their briefcases and luggage from the overhead bins. Sharon wondered what each of them was thinking. She wondered where they were heading to. All these people had just shared two hours of their lives with her and that would be it. She would most likely never see any one of them ever again. She watched through the window as the airport workers unloaded the bags from the plane. A few minutes later, new faces would come and take the same seats for the rest of the journey. An elderly woman walked slowly toward her, pausing to look at her ticket and then glancing up to see if she was at the right spot.

"Miss, is my seat next to you?" She hands her ticket to Sharon. Sharon took the ticket and saw that the woman was assigned to the seat next to her.

"Yes, this is the right place!" Sharon said smiling.

"Oh, thank goodness. I was so hoping this would be easy! Said the woman.

She sat in her seat and placed a large colorful straw bag on the floor, the kind that doubles as a purse and a shopping bag.

"My name is Millie, what's yours?" asked the woman.

"I'm Sharon. Pleased to meet you."

"So nice to meet you." Said the woman. "I'm going to Miami to visit my daughter."

"Well that's nice. I'm heading to the Cayman Islands on business. My daughter is going to join me later."

Sharon listened as Millie talked about her daughter and the good time she was planning to have with her. Millie talked about her life as a young woman and how quickly time passes. Soon she fell asleep.

A few hours later the pilot announced they were approaching their destination. The passengers, with the assistance of the stewards, put their tray tables up and picked up trash. The captain of the Boeing 747 banked the giant craft slightly and leveled the plane just as it passed over the shoreline. Sharon could see the shadow of the jet below on the beach as they approached the Owen Roberts International Airport. She helped Millie with her things and the two of them made their way down the tight, crowded aisle of the plane, through the airway and into the terminal.

"Well, thank you for the nice conversation and the help you've given me Sharon. Sorry about falling to sleep on you," Millie said.

"Oh, I'm so glad to have met you. I think I nodded off too," Sharon said laughing. Sharon gave Millie a little hug. "I hate to say goodbye, so here's my business card. If you ever need any legal help, or you just want to say hello, give me a call."

"Thank you dear," Millie said, taking the card. "Oh, there's my daughter. Guess I'd better go now. Take care and have fun. Bye!" Millie waved to Sharon as she walked toward her daughter. She waved to Sharon again as they walked out of the terminal and out of sight. Sharon spotted her luggage circling on the baggage carousel. She picks it up and pulls out the handle towing it behind her as she walked out the airport's automatic glass doors.

26

The trucker gazed out of the window of the New Orleans Greyhound bus station. He had managed to travel from New Hampshire to Louisiana in just two days. He traveled light, with only a backpack to carry his few personal belongings. He was tired today. He takes out an old flip cell phone from his jeans pocket to check the time. Hunger was calling him. He looks around and spots a small doughnut and coffee shop across the street. The trucker picks up his backpack and walks briskly through the doors of the bus station and out onto Loyola avenue. The warm rays of the Louisiana sun warmed his face. It felt good to be out of the hard cold of the Northeast. The trucker walked several blocks before he came upon Mother's Restaurant on Poydras street. He was hungry now and the array of Creole delicacies made his stomach growl. He ordered a big bowl of seafood and okra gumbo and two Benets dusted with powdered sugar. The old restaurant was always crowded. The trucker found a seat towards the back and settled in to enjoy the best food he had eaten since that evening in the little cafe back east. He thought about Karen's pecan pie, took a big bite of a Benet and washed it down with some black Community coffee. He spied a copy of the morning Times-Picayune down the counter. The front page was full of the news for the day, which he had already absorbed from the flat screens in the bus station and the one hanging in the corner of the coffee shop. He was about to move on to the sports section when he paused for a small headline.

Kansas City Police Search for Missing Truck Driver.

"Would you like a warmup?"

The man looked briefly at the young woman holding a pot of coffee. Then he looked back at the newspaper.

"Yes, can I have it to go?" he said.

The trucker looked up again. The young woman was about 35 years old he thought. She had on a white linen sleeveless blouse that complimented her tan freckled skin. Her brunette-red hair was pulled back into a long ponytail that draped over her left shoulder.

"Thanks. Is there a motel or something close by? Nothing special, I just need a place to get some rest for a day or so."

"What's your name?" she asked with a kind of quizzical look on her face, half serious, half curious. He paused for a moment.

"Ted, my name is Ted."

"I don't know, but you don't look like a Ted." She said with a smirk.

"I don't?" He hadn't expected her to say that.

"Okay, what's *your* name?"

"Suzanne, do I sound like a Suzanne?"

"That's fair, I like it." He said.

"There's an old hotel two blocks down the street. Hotel Monteleone." She pointed the direction. The coffee shop was getting busy. Suzanne started pouring coffee and helping other customers. A few minutes later, she saw Ted getting up from the table.

If you get a chance, come back and visit before you move on." She said.

"Okay, I will." The trucker rolled up the newspaper, threw the backpack over his shoulder and headed up the busy street in the direction Suzanne had pointed.

27

Josh and Bill made the trip back to Manchester and checked into a Marriott for the evening.

"I think I'm going to check on things in the office and take a short nap. We can figure out what we are going to do later if that's okay with you." Said Bill.

"Sounds good, I need to check with Lace and see how things are going with a case she's working on. He looked at his watch. It was almost three o'clock in the afternoon. See you around five," said Josh.

Josh slid his feet out of his sneakers and stretched out on the bed. He didn't bother to call Lace. He knew she would take care of her end. Josh pulled his ball cap over his eyes and slipped into a soft sleep.

"Run Josh, run boy!" Josh could hear the voice somewhere in the distance. He could feel his heart come to life as the blood flowed faster. He wasn't tired, he had run harder than this before, but there was an unfamiliar urgency in the voice. The night air was crisp, and he could smell the scent of water. Josh ran across the landscape along an old bayou where ancient Cypress trees posed along the bank. Their ancient roots holding the ground like old arthritic hands gripping the soil. He ran, ran up and down the countryside of wherever he was. He didn't know. The fading sunlight made it difficult to see. Then he heard a what sounded like a gunshot. The

sound startled him. He pulls the cap from his brow and sat up in the bed. His heart was still racing, and the hotel room was momentarily disorienting. A few seconds later, his cell phone signaled a text message was waiting. It was from Speight.

Please call me when you get a chance.

Josh looks at his watch. It was almost four o'clock now. He could see the setting sun from the hotel window. He called Speight but got no answer. He didn't bother leaving a message. He and the cop had spoken often enough since the crash. Speight would see that he had missed the call and call back. Josh didn't want to disturb Bill just yet, so he called Lace, but she didn't answer either. He left a message for her to call when she could. He would call Sharon late or maybe tomorrow. He figured she was still getting settled in from the long trip. She always called after arriving at a destination.

Josh watched the winter sun burn the snowy landscape as it settled below the eastern horizon. The sun cast an orange glow against the blue evening sky. A scant white fluff of clouds from The Artist's pallet. Josh imagined a huge ball of steam billowing up from the ground as that white, hot orb settled in for the night. But that didn't happen. There was a knock on the door.

"Hey, you still snoozing in there?" said Bill. Josh rolled off the bed and opened the door.

"Nah, I've been awake for a while. I made a couple of phone calls, but everybody was busy. That cop text me to call him, but his didn't pick up when I called him," said Josh.

"He'll call back soon. Hope he's got something we can get our noses on."

Josh's cell phone rings.

"Speight, what's up?"

"We got a couple of phone calls from New Orleans PD. We aren't really hot about either of them. Still following up for more info. There's a woman there who saw a newspaper article about our guy. She thinks she saw him. We're trying to get more info through the NOPD."

"That's kind of a weak lead isn't it?" asked Josh. "A newspaper article in the New Orleans newspaper?"

"I know, the article didn't have a lot of detail. Kind of one of those "in other news" things, but it seems our case got some legs. All news travels somewhere I guess. But we've got to chase it down. If we learn anything else that I can share with you, I'll let you know."

"Bill and I will be on the ground in New Orleans tomorrow."

"Fine, you have an informal clearance. The department knows you are working privately. I don't have to remind you some of the guys aren't particularly fond of P.I's, even if they are former cops."

"Thanks Speight for the warning, occupational hazard I guess," Josh laughed.

"We'll talk later," said Speight. The call ended.

"So, when you want to ride like the wind!?" Bill said excitedly.

"Man, I haven't heard anyone use that term in a long time, except my Dad," said Josh.

"I'm an old soul Josh," said Bill.

"There's no sense in leaving now, in the dark. Let's just rest here tonight and hit it tomorrow at first light."

"Okay, let's grab some breakfast first. We'll need some time anyway to get the plane fueled," said Bill.

"I want you to know, I'm starting to gain some weight traveling with you," Josh said with a grin.

28

It was Sunday, football day. Warren James flips through the channels on the curved screen television suspended on a wall built with natural blocks of granite. The stones chiseled and placed so the wall seemed to have always been part of the floor it was built on. The top of the wall stretched to the ceiling and melted away, giving the effect that this modern cave had always been there. The bar blended into one of the cave walls and was illuminated by a soft white light. Rows of bourbon, scotch, vodka and gin sat neatly organized on glass shelves anchored to a mirrored wall. A large tinted plate glass window provided a view of a small lake. A little canoe was tied to a single wooden dock, waiting for someone to come put it away for the winter. Warren James poured a couple shots of bourbon over a single oversized cube of ice and sat it down on a table that stood next to a large leather chair. It was the playoffs in the NFL. He couldn't help but think about the missing truck driver. He didn't know the man at all. He knew nothing about him, this Jackson Mann. The name didn't matter, what mattered was that was one of his men remained out of control and on the loose. He picked up the crystal cocktail glass and took a swallow of the chilled bourbon. The alcohol soothed his throat and warmed his body. The anxiety lifted a little and things didn't seem quite so unmanageable.

"Honey, are you in there?" said Marie.

"Yeah, I'm here. Just watching some football. Are you coming to join me?"

"Sure, maybe for a little while." Marie settled in the matching leather chair next to her husband. "Who's playing today? I've lost track since the playoffs started."

"The Chiefs play next week, so no worries for now."

"That's good, I guess," Marie noticed a slight distance in his voice. "So, how is the hunt for that driver going? What's his name anyway?

"Jackson Mann. His name is Jackson Mann. George confirmed the name for me."

"George, at the office?" asked Marie.

"Yeah. He says he might be headed to Florida, or maybe try to disappear in New York. We guess it's probably Florida." It's much easier to be on the run when its warm. I need to get control of this real soon!" said Warren James.

"You will dear, just relax. You can't control everything all at once, said Marie with a smile. "Okay, what's it going to be for dinner tonight? Are we going out, or is one of us going to cook?"

"We both know you are the better cook."

"Let's go out. I don't feel like cooking today," said Marie.

"I'll get dressed and we can go."

Warren heard the ring of his cell phone as he came out of the shower. He dried himself with an oversized white bath towel and picked up the phone on what was probably the last ring.

"Hello." He pulled a heavy shower robe over his shoulders. He couldn't help but notice how it made him look like a boxer. At least he thought so.

"Warren James, this is Detective Speight."

"Detective Speight, did you get a promotion?"

"You are observant, Mr. James. Yes, I did," replied the detective." We think Jackson Mann is in New Orleans."

"Really? We were thinking Florida."

"Can you tell me anything else about the delivery van left at the motel?"

"Not really." Warren James wasn't sure what he would say if he did know something.

"Okay, Mr. James. I have a call waiting. I'll stay in contact. Have a good day."

"Of course, detective, you have a good day as well." Warren James ended the call.

29

Lace Benton examines the little crow's feet in the corners of her eyes. She brushes her hair back and touches the skin around her neck and ears, looking for moles, freckles, anything that would suggest time might be catching up to her, closing the gap on her youthful look and age. She brushes on some foundation, covering a line on the right cheek. She pauses a moment. It was ever so slight she thought. The words of an old Eagles song came to her:

> There were lines in the mirror, lines on her face
> She pretended not to notice, she was caught up in the race

Today is going to be a good day. I've got plenty of time to slow down. Lace thought to herself.

She was meeting with the old man and Natalie today. She had arranged a meeting for the reunion at one of the hotels on The Country Club Plaza. She decided a casual friendly look would be good for her job today. She selected a simple white cotton blouse, a pair of denim jeans and an old pair of cowgirl boots from her closet.

Natalie stood on the sidewalk at the Southwest terminal of the Mid-Continent International airport. Lace was maneuvering the black Corvette through traffic when she spotted Natalie wearing the purple ski jacket she said she would wear. Lace pulls the car to the curb, stopped and rolled down the window.

"Hey Natalie, just pull back the seat and throw your luggage back there. You can't hurt anything, there's nothing back there except maybe my old jeans!"

Natalie laughed and placed a well-traveled leather bag behind the seat before climbing into the Corvette. Lace pulled away from the curb, slowly working her way through the parade of cars picking up and dropping off loved ones and business travelers.

"Thanks for picking me up. It's been a long day,". Natalie said with a sigh of relief. "I haven't seen or spoken to my father in a long time, too long I suppose." Natalie paused, peering out of the window as Lace pushes the Corvette along the interstate toward the landscape of the city. "But, I'm excited to see him, I guess. Now that I'm older, maybe wiser I suppose, I can see things differently. When I was younger, things seemed to be easier to place, easier to organize into nice squares and holes. My father was a good provider. He worked all the time to support us. My mom was as good a mother as she knew how to be, but she needed help sometimes."

Lace nodded her head, so Natalie would know she was listening.

"I've had some time to think about this since you first contacted me about my father. He wasn't the most graceful person. Despite his successes, he was still just a common man. He didn't understand. Back then, when I was a kid, people just didn't understand some things."

"What kinds of things?" asked Lace.

"You know, girl stuff. When I got older, things seem to change between them. I don't know…I'm sorry, I didn't mean to get so serious.

"That's okay, I get it. So, your dad got frustrated and bolted?"

"Something like that. Anyway, it's time to let the bad stuff go. Not easy to do, but it's time." Lace gave the keys to the valet and the two women walked into the Raphael Hotel. The manager was checking Natalie into her room when the elevator door opened. Natalie looked at the man standing in the elevator. The old man stood motionless as the memories of his daughter struggled to match the young, but mature woman standing in front of him. Lace walked over to the man, taking his hand.

"Mr. Garibaldi, this is your daughter Natalie." The father and daughter were visibly nervous and awkward. The father held out his hand. Natalie took her father's hand and held it nervously, trying to decide what to do next. Her father stood there smiling and opened his arms for a hug…and they hugged. Lace had made reservations for the three of them in the hotel restaurant and the evening went smoothly, with Lace acting as host and ice breaker for the two. She hadn't expected to become so personally involved with this project Josh had given her, but now she was having fun and feeling connected to something exceptionally good today. She had reconnected a family member and hopefully healed some old wounds.

Later, that evening Lace was back at home working on the computer. She had handled one of the jobs Josh had asked her to do, now she was going to focus on the shipping case. She had already spent a lot of time getting acquainted with the trucking industry. She decided to focus on shipping. She found a report on a website about international cargo shipping. There were photos of different types of cargo ships, both small and large. Then she saw it. In one of the photos was a small ship with the letters *Daimler* on its bow.

30

The morning stars dimmed in the eastern sky as the night gave way to the blue of morning. Bill and Josh walk into the airport café and take a seat at the counter. The small airport was located near New Orleans International. It was old, but still functional. The café succeeded with its fifties theme and looked as if the decorators had decided to run with the look, spiffing it up with rebirth décor. There was jukebox standing in the corner near the window. An old poster of Rocking Sidney Simien and his Zydeco band hung over it. Close by was that classic picture of James Dean, Marilyn Monroe, and Elvis Presley sitting at that bar in the early hours of the morning when most people are still sleeping. A woman walked out of the kitchen behind the counter. She was short in stature and wore a blue denim dress draped with a faded white apron. Her graying hair was pulled back into a bun. She dried her wet hands with an old white dish towel and threw it over her left shoulder.

"Can I get you boys some breakfast this morning?" She smiled, her blue eyes twinkled as if Josh and Bill were her own sons, if she had any.

"Just some coffee, please." said Josh. "Two coffees to go."

The woman brought the coffee. Bill laid a five-dollar bill on the counter. "Keep the change." said Bill.

They pick up the two cups of coffee and took the elevator from the café down to street level. The door opened into a shiny hallway of marble and windows and polished brass. They follow the signs pointing the way to the exit onto Airline street.

"Refresh my memory," said Bill. "Where are we going?"

"To talk to our contact. The one who reported seeing the trucker. Her name is Suzanne. She works at a restaurant near a bus station. So, let's figure out where the bus station is and go there. Google it and let's go from there.

The Palms Cafe was busy with lunch hour customers. Bill and Josh make their way through the courtyard and sit at a table near the outdoor bar. Soon a waitress comes with two glasses filled with iced water and menus."

"What can I get you two for lunch?"

"Not sure yet, give us a minute to look it over. Are you Suzanne?" asks Josh.

"Maybe, who wants to know?"

"I'm Josh Landry. I'm a private investigator. This is my associate Bill Haas."

"I suppose you are here about that guy the police are looking for right?" The waitress looks at Josh and the Bill.

Yes, we are," says Josh.

"I don't know what else I can tell you I haven't already told your buddies. He came in here, we chatted a little, he ordered something and left."

"Did he say anything about where he was going?" asked Bill.

"He wanted to know about a place to stay. I told him about an old hotel, not too far from her. It's called The Monteleone. It's just a couple blocks down the street." Suzanne said, pointing the direction of the hotel. "Nice to meet you, I've got to get busy again. I'll come back to take your order if you want anything."

Josh and Bill both order turkey and swiss sandwiches. They eat quickly and Suzanne for the check. "Here's my card if anything else comes to mind. Maybe we'll stop by later," Said Josh.

"That's what the guy you're looking for said when he left." Suzanne said with a smile as she walked away.

31

Sharon was tired when she finally arrived at Jason and Delores little Georgetown beach home. Jason helped her with the luggage while Delores excitedly showed Sharon the small bedroom in the back of the house where she would stay for the next few days. Sharon had reserved a room at one of the hotels, but Delores insisted she at least stay a couple of days with them.

"We don't get a lot of visitors from back home, except for Rene...and that's not often. My, that company you work for sure keeps the two of you busy!" We just don't see enough of you girls," said Delores."

"Delores brings that up all the time," said Jason."

"Well, it's true. I miss my girls!" Delores replied, giving Sharon a big hug.

"I always tell her we can move back home. That way we would have more time with everybody," said Jason.

"It's too cold at home," said Delores, crossing her arms to protect against just the thought of it.

"And there you have it," said Jason.

"I love you guys, thanks for inviting me to stay. I'm sure Rene will be her sometime this week," said Sharon.

"I talked to Madeline yesterday. We may have one more coming to the party!" Delores was gleaming.

"My mother is coming too? She never mentioned that," said Sharon.

"I think she realized she was going to be alone while she was helping Savannah get packed."

Well, I suppose I need to finish my work here before the party starts, "Sharon said. "I can move to a hotel or something nearby, so it won't be crowded."

"No dear, we will find room for everyone right here. You'll see, it'll be fun."

Sharon walks down the narrow wood floor hallway and into the bedroom where Jason had set her luggage.

"Towels are in the little closet next to the sink," Delores yelled from the kitchen.

A little window with white French shutters faced the foot of the old bronze wrought iron bed. Sharon watched the seagulls diving and darting in the distant sky as a peaceful rest found its way to her bedside. She slept well that night. She dreamed she was with Savannah and Ali walking on a beach somewhere, flying kites, splashing along the water's edge, sand between their toes, the sun bright and warm. The sisters laughing and playing. A gentle breeze rattled the old wooden shutters, waking Sharon from her sleep. Morning had come. The rest had done her good. Bring on the day. Today she would call Josh. She hadn't spoken to him since he and Bill flew to Manchester. Sharon showered, dressed and walks toward the kitchen where Delores was baking something in the oven.

32

Josh and Bill made their way to the Monteleone Hotel on Canal street near the French Quarter. The receptionist couldn't find anyone registered there under the name of Jackson Mann, but Josh didn't expect it would be that easy anyway, so they decided to check in to a room and spend the night there observing for any signs the trucker might still be there. It was a slow uneventful evening. Bill was busy on the phone returning calls to customers while Josh takes periodic walks around the hotel property watching for any sign of the trucker. Later that night, Josh observes someone at the far edge of the rear parking area. A small dark colored sedan was parked in the shadow of the halogen parking lamps. Josh grabs a pair of binoculars from his travel bag. He could see a short, slender man open the trunk of the car and place some boxes in it, but he couldn't see clearly what those boxes contained because the car was parked facing out, the rear of the car partially hidden because of the angle.

"What you see out there Josh? Looks like you're studying something'," said Bill.

"Not sure. Can you see that guy out there way in the back just to the right of the light?" Josh hands Bill the binoculars, pointing out the direction.

"Yeah, I see him. What do you think?" asked Bill, handing the binoculars back to Josh.

"I think I'm going to take a little evening walk in that direction."

"Okay, I'll watch from here," said Bill.

\   Josh slips on a jacket and grabs his Smith & Wesson 9mm from a leather travel bag, placing it neatly into an inside chest pocket of the jacket. He opens the door of the hotel room and walks briskly down the hallway passing the elevator toward the exit sign at the far end of the hall. Josh descends the stairway three flights to the main floor and out the side entry of the hotel. He walks around to the rear of the building to the parking lot. He can still see the interior light of the dark sedan. Josh walks casually toward the man now sitting in the car. As he gets closer, Josh can see the man wearing a ball cap and reading something on his cell phone. A white Toyota is parked next to the dark sedan. The man in the car looks up and sees Josh stop next to the white Toyota. Josh pretends to fumble for his keys.

"Damn it, left the keys in my room! Josh spoke loud enough for the stranger to hear, hoping he wouldn't get suspicious. Using this temporary cover, Josh tries to observe anything unusual about this stranger. Their eyes meet for a moment. The stranger gets out of his car. Josh's cell phone lights up, announcing a call from Lace Benton. He lets the call go to voicemail.

"Well, I guess I still need to get my keys," said Josh, still trying to be casual. "How's your evening going?" Josh asked the stranger.

"Okay I guess." The man's voice was guarded.

"Nice hotel. You stay here often? Josh asked.

"No, first time. How about you?" The man had turned to face Josh now, eyes looking away.

Josh could see a brochure on the backseat of the man's car. It was like the one he and Bill saw in the white van back in New Hampshire. He could barely make out the word Cayman. He could also see the words Freeport and a few others, but it was dark, and the parking lot lights weren't enough to see clearly. By then, the man had looked up and could see Josh staring into his car.

"Well, I need to get going," the slender man said.

He turned quickly, opens the car door and drives away. Josh memorizes the license plate number as the sedan slowly made its way out of the parking lot. Josh decides to follow the car. He waits until the car got far enough away so the stranger couldn't see the headlights of Josh's car in case he was watching. Josh called Bill and told him he was following the stranger. Bill stayed at the hotel as a lookout in case the stranger returned to the hotel.

Josh follows the sedan through downtown and along Canal street and on toward Interstate 55 as it made its way west. The two cars traveled west about twenty-five miles until a sign announced the exit at I-10 and Airline Highway to LaPlace, Louisiana. Josh follows the sedan off the exit and around the curve. In the dark, he could barely see the sign that said he was at The Port of South Louisiana. Several cargo ships and barges were docked up and down the port. The car turned left and slowly approached the pier where a smaller, inconspicuous vessel was anchored. It was loaded with several containers bearing the Daimler 8 logo. Josh found a place to stop a safe distance away and turned off the headlights. The lights of a minivan flashed twice. The stranger got out of the car, walked toward the minivan and got in. Josh called Bill on his cell phone.

"Bill, I followed this guy down to the Port about twenty-five miles from her in LaPlace and guess what we have here?"

"I give up, tell me!

"There's a cargo ship here with several containers with Daimler 8 on them!"

"Okay Josh, I don't need to tell you to be careful. I can grab one of the hotel loaners and meet you out there! Said Bill.

"Good idea, just in case. I 've got to get closer, maybe try to talk with these guys, so I'll stay put and give you some time to get here before I make a move. There are at least two more people in a minivan joining the party." Said Josh.

"Heading your way now, text you when I get there."

Josh watches the van for several minutes before deciding to get closer. He slips out of the car and stays in the shadows as he made his way closer to the van. A few moments later the door opened and two of the men got out. He could barely hear them talking, but he could see them pointing toward the ship. Josh stayed crouched in the darkness behind a parked pickup, moving closer so he could hear better. Bill text he had arrived and was parked near

Josh's car where he could see the men and the minivan. Josh text Bill...

Thinking about walking up on these guys. What do you think?

Well, we ain't exactly the cops, so I guess we go for it. I'm ready.

Josh doubled checked his 9mm and walked out of the shadows towards the men.

33

David Cavanaugh put the key in the lock of the hotel door. His flight from Kansas City had been without event, but he was tired. He drew back the sheers from the French windows looking out at the beach across the street from the little bungalow. David preferred smaller boutique style hotels over the accommodations of the big chains. Rene would always book them for him if a good one was available. It was still afternoon as David stretched out across the fluffy bed. The mattress was comfortable enough. He sat up on the bed and pulled a pair of ear buds and an iPad from his briefcase laying on the small antique desk in the corner of the room.

Sharon called David's cell phone three times, with no answer, before she called Rene to check on him. Rene gave her the name and telephone number of the hotel. The flashing lights on the hotel phone set finally got his attention.

"Hello." David answered.

"David, why aren't you answering your cell phone?"

"I'm sorry Sharon, I was listening to a program on the iPad. Sorry, I didn't think about it."

"We have a meeting tomorrow with representatives of the Governor's public relations team."

"Fine, what time is the meeting?"

"First thing in the morning, nine o'clock." Said Sharon.

"Well then, I suppose we ought to get together and consider what we're going to say," said David. "Usually in these political scenarios somebody has some dirty laundry. Maybe we can find some of Johnathan Hatch's."

"Dirty laundry?" Queried Sharon."

"Well, yes, it might result in that, but I think we should approach our client about what they know about the security of international shipments coming to the Caymans. Test the water first and see if any rats jump overboard." David smiled, amused with his comment.

"Okay, how about we meet at your hotel in the morning for coffee. I'm staying at Rene's folks place tonight. I'll grab a taxi and meet you there about seven o'clock?"

"Fine, I think I might stay in for dinner tonight and catch up on some things. I'll see you in the morning."

The next morning the taxi driver drove them to the Government Administration building in downtown Georgetown. Sharon's cell phone rang. She didn't recognize the number.

"Hello."

"Sharon, this is Lace Benton, you remember we met once?"

"Yes, I remember. You knew Josh way back when. How can I help you?"

"I've been trying to help Josh find the trucker seems everyone is looking for. He asked me to find some information on some organization called Daimler."

"Okay, he hadn't shared that with me, but go on."

"Well, I learned a lot just doing the research including some interesting political ties to the Caymans. I called your office, about it before calling your cell. Anyway, it appears that some politician there has a stake in that Daimler company."

Sharon turns her phone to speakerphone, so David could hear the conversation.

"Who is the politician with the ties to Daimler?" Sharon asked?

"Hold on a minute, let me pull it up." A few seconds passed. "Johnathan Hatch. Looks like he's a big stakeholder according to this." Said Lace Benton. "You want me to send the link?"

"Absolutely, if you don't mind!"

"Okay, I'll text it to you. Good talking to you again Sharon. I haven't forgotten about Ali. Let me know if I can do anything more. You've got my number now."

"Thanks Lace. Bye."

David and Sharon looked at each other.

"Well, if I heard that correctly, I think we have a little something to add to our meeting today." Said David.

Sharon and David Cavanaugh were greeted by a staff member and led to one of the small meeting rooms near the

Governor's office. There were four members of the Cayman government waiting for them. A woman in her late forties walked briskly across the room, a welcome hand extended to David and Sharon. Her skin was dark and smooth like a polished black pearl. Her eyes full and glowing inside a sharply chiseled face. She reminded David of an African warrior queen. He was already an admirer of her ancient beauty. He guessed she was of Ethiopian descent. Her long black, silky hair seemed to flow as she moved toward them.

"Please come in and good morning! My name is Jane Cooling and I am the Governor's Personal Assistant. We are delighted to spend this time with you. Please help yourself to the coffee and breakfast items. Let's start the morning with refreshments and settle into discussion, shall we?" David began the discussion. "Ms. Cooling, are you aware of any unusual shipments coming to the island?" David had a natural presence when he was in a room and particularly if he had an audience. He wasn't particularly tall or athletic, but he carried himself in a manner that got attention. A pleasant and engaging personality, he spoke with a smooth baritone voice that focused the attention of his listener.

"Please, call me Jane. No, not that I'm aware of."

"Our company, Cavanaugh International, does ongoing research and analysis on a variety of topics regarding international trade. We have information suggesting there is a high probability some of that trade is illegal and a lot of it is concentrated in the Caribbean and not just The Caymans.

"Well, we are extremely interested in learning of more about this activity. Particularly since the Governor is facing some heat from the opposition," said Jane.

"You mean Jonathan Hatch. Yes, we thought about that. We are almost certain Mr. Hatch is central to our investigation."

"You think Hatch is smuggling drugs or something?"

"No, I don't. But I think he is aware of this trade activity and is spinning it to his advantage. Let me explain further," said David pausing to loosen his tie. "There is always a small amount of undocumented trade going on all over the world. Even though it is technically illegal, doesn't necessarily mean that the goods being transported are necessarily bad. Everything isn't about heroin or marijuana, or drugs in general for that matter. A lot of it is just plain everyday stuff like vitamins, aspirin, herbal supplements, etcetera."

"But some of it could be bad product couldn't it?" asked Jane.

"Of course, I'm not discounting that point. From a larger perspective, it is alarming from another perspective. Case in point," David turns and points to Sharon. My colleague lost a child in a semi-tractor trailer accident involving a driver involved down the line in this illegal trade. He's probably just trying to make a living and maybe, but Sharon lost her child as a result. But in your case, that's not the real issue.

"Okay, then what is it then?"

"It's quite simple really. Johnathan Hatch is taking this small fact of reality and spinning it into something larger. He's taking something the public is unaware of and makes it a larger issue. He then turns around and lays it at the foot of the Governor."

"So, how do we fix that?"

"We have intel that says Johnathan Hatch is a player in that trade. He owns a large stake in a shipping firm called Daimler 8. So, here's what you do. We start a campaign that implies this information. We hold back on most of the facts and release them to the press as we go along. First, we make people aware of the stuff they don't know about cargo, shipping and so on. Then we start to talk about Daimler 8 and continue the build until we tag Mr. Hatch. He will probably disappear from the radar before we get all the way along."

"I like it," said Jane Cooling. "Let's do it.

34

"Anybody here know Jackson Mann?!" Josh yelled to the three men. The men turned toward the direction of the voice and froze. Josh was still camouflaged by the night's shadows preventing the trio from seeing him clearly.

"Who wants to know?" replied one of the men. "Show yourself, we're getting a little nervous over here."

Josh stepped from behind the pickup and into the dull light of the parking lot.

"Okay, can you see me now? I asked if any of you know a man by the name of Jackson Mann?"

"Are you the Coast Guard or something?"

"Not exactly, my name is Joshua Landry. My friends call me Josh, but you can call me whatever you want. It really doesn't matter!" Josh said, stepping up the tone. "I'm a private investigator and I'm looking for Jackson Mann!" The sound of those words at that moment didn't ring true to Josh. He had announced himself as a P.I. many times before, but now he didn't feel like one.

Bill was still inside the car, watching the action through a pair of night vision binoculars from about 30 yards away. He could see the smaller cargo ship drop its dock ties and slowly back away from the pier. At the same moment one of the men bolted away from the van running toward the pier. Josh pursued him as the minivan began to move across the parking lot. Bill turns on the headlights of his car and starts across the lot to cut the van off. The man ran down the boardwalk with Josh in hot pursuit. They eventually run off the boardwalk and onto the ground along the Mississippi. The terrain eventually gave way to rock and dirt as the pursuit led to higher ground and away from the river. Josh guessed they had already run a good half mile. He was certain he was chasing Jackson Mann. They came through a patch of Palmetto trees and wetland. The air was cooler than normal, but the humidity made breathing a little harder. They were both starting to tire. Josh pushed on slowly, closing the distance on his prey. Then they hit a smooth stretch of ground. The chase continued as Jackson Mann picked up the pace. Josh hadn't run this far over natural ground in a long time. His mind was racing with the beating of his heart. He thought of his days as a boy running on his grandparent's farm.

Run Josh. Run boy! Breathe deep. Run Josh!

His grandfather's voice. Those summer days at the old farm deep in the Louisiana Bayou. Now the adrenaline kicked in. Josh was within one hundred feet of his prey. Jackson Mann looked back. Josh was dead on him. His heart screaming, he knew he had to stop.

"A bit chilly out here for an August night, don't you think?" He said bent over, trying to catch his breath, hands resting on his knees, heart racing.

"I suppose that depends on how you like to spend your summer nights," said Josh.

"So, what do we do now?" said Jackson Mann. He was starting to breathe easier now. "You got the advantage, what's your move?"

"Hell, I don't know just yet. What's the rush, we've been at this for several months now." Josh's voice was low and menacing. He was angry. The reality of why he was standing on a southern Louisiana port facing off with three men and chasing one of them for over a mile came home to him. He felt a greater deeper, primal force well up inside.

Josh watched as Jackson Mann stood up.

"Keep your hands high," said Josh. His gun drawn, the laser sighted Smith & Wesson 9mm painted a red dot on the man's temple.

"I don't have a gun Mr. Landry. Please don't shoot. I don't blame you for being angry." He was starting to shiver, the perspiration started to chill his body in the night air. Josh felt it too.

"Why shouldn't I? You killed my little girl."

The shadows became one with the night. The sound of waves rushed against the shore below like a Shakespearean chorus chanting a foreboding rhythm. Josh squeezed the trigger. The Shrill cries of Seagulls taking flight swallowed up the sharp crack of gunfire.

35

Jason and Delores were waiting on the porch when the taxi pulled into the drive. Jason walks over to the car as Savannah jumped out and gave him a bug hug and then another hug for Delores.

"It's so good to see you Savannah, you are almost a woman now!" Said Delores.

"My, you and Jason look great!" said Madeline with a big smile. "How long has it been since I last laid eyes on you two?"

"We can add up the months later, come on inside! Delores was beaming She loved house guests.

The driver, a young man in his early thirties helped Jason bring the luggage into the house. He wore a sleeveless Bob Marley t-shirt, a pair of cut up jeans and a well-worn pair of Sketchers on his feet. He sported a neatly groomed crown of dreadlocks. Jason liked the young man's courtesy.

"So, do you stay busy driving around the island?" Jason asked.

"Yes sir, I do fine. I work for myself right now, man. I think I can make a go of it if I can maybe buy another car. Ya' know, maybe hire another driver."

Jason gave the young man a twenty-dollar bill for a tip.

"Thank you, sir, have a good day.

Jason turns and walks toward the porch. The young man honked as he pulled away from the cottage. Jason gave him a "thumbs up" as the car drove away. Inside everyone was still hugging and laughing. Delores was busy making coffee and cutting pound cake for anyone who wanted some."

"So, when is Rene coming?" asked Delores

"She's right behind us on a later flight. I think she should be here shortly before we go to bed. I'm so excited I don't think I can sleep anyway!" said Madeline.

"You think I could keep up with the whereabouts of my own daughter, now wouldn't you? Lord, I must be getting old!" Said Delores, smiling as she set out napkins and silverware. Savannah was busy with her computer tablet when she saw Sharon walk in the door shortly after Jason.

"Hey Mommy, I'm so glad to see you!"

The two of them hug and they all celebrate the evening sunset on the island.

36

Josh was still holding his gun on Jackson Mann.

"So, are you going to kill me, or just take some pot shots at me?"

"Hmmm, I don't know. I'm still thinking about it. It might depend on what you say I guess," said Josh.

"On what I have to say? What do you want me to say!? You want me to say I'm sorry? Okay, I'm sorry."

"I don't think that was sincere enough," said Josh, quietly holding his aim. "What were you and your friends doing at the docks?"

Jackson Mann was silent.

"You know, I really don't want to stand out here all night, so you better tell me something. I don't really have a great need to especially nice to you tonight!"

Jackson Mann sensed from Josh's tone that he better get real.

"What is the deal with the crash back in Missouri and you being on these docks tonight? I'm giving you another five minutes to tell me something!"

Josh saw the man turn his head to the right. Josh looks in the same direction, still holding the gun. It was Bill walking toward them.

"You two boys get tired of running yet?" Bill chuckled as he stood next to Josh. "I finally found you, compliments of a little satellite homing signal in your cell phone, my friend. That gunshot helped a lot too."

"I was just asking our friend here about his business. He was just about to tell me something I think.

"I'm not telling you guys shit. Just call the goddamn police will ya'. You got me."

Bill looked at Josh and then turned his gaze back to Jackson Mann, still sitting on the ground.

"Well, my friend it's kind of like this. You see, sometimes we like to know about stuff before the police do. I'm sure you know what I mean. It's sort of how my friend here makes a living." Bill knelt next to the man and looked him in the face. "Now the way I see this situation, you're in kind of a pickle. My friend here lost his baby girl because of you. We're both a little tired from chasing you around the last few weeks. I got a business to run and we both want to go home. Now I don't give a rat's ass if my friend here puts one right between your eyes. We'll call the police after that. When they show up, we'll tell them about the little cross-country race you and Josh participated in and we'll tell em' about that boat with Daimler written on the side pulling out of the harbor. Police already know we out here helping them find you and we know you got a bad rap sheet." Bill paused a minute, still looking Jackson Mann in the eyes. "So, the way I figure it, you and Josh here got into it before I got here. You pulled a gun and Josh had to defend himself. Bang, you're dead!"

"I told you I don't have a gun!"

Bill pulled a small caliber pistol from his jacket and placed it on the ground between the two of them. "Yes, you do."

Jackson Mann paused a moment, letting Bill's words sink in. Then he told Josh and Bill about his ties to the Daimler organization. He described how he drove trucks for the Caribbean based company shipping prescription drugs and other sundry medical products not approved by governments. He told them he usually knew what he was carrying, but sometimes there were shipments he did not know about.

"I smoked a joint in the truck not more than thirty minutes earlier. I got paranoid and ran. Stupid, I should have played it cool. All my paperwork was in order."

"What do you know about Warren James?" asked Josh.

"He's the man."

"I know that, but does he know about this Daimler shipping thing!"

"I don't know. He might know about it, but I really don't know for sure. I'm just a runner they don't involve me in the decision making. Look guys, I got a family too, just like you.

"Maybe you do and maybe you don't," said Josh. "I've got to tell you, you don't seem like the kind of guy who would have a family and if you do, I'd say they deserve better."

"So, what's your move Josh. I say we just shoot em'!" Bill was laughing.

"Don't tempt me."

37

Warren James sits in a meeting with the members of the international Brotherhood of Teamsters. It had been a long time since he sat at the same table with people like himself. A steadfast union supporter and organizer, the Company recognized his leadership skill, tapping him for a managing position before the union could get a grip on him. The union still respected him and still considered him one of their own. The discussion turned to rogue drivers in the organization and the negative impact they had on the industry when an office assistant brought James a memo. Written on a little sticky note...*call Detective Speight.*

"Excuse me gentlemen, I need to make a phone call. Let's take lunch now, it's almost that time anyway. I'll join you shortly."

Warren James waits until everyone has left the room before making the call to Detective Speight.

"Thanks for calling me back so quickly, Mr. James."

"No problem, what's going on?"

"I wanted you to know that Josh Landry has tracked down Jackson Mann in New Orleans."

"I see, well that's good news I guess."

"I will be in contact later, once we have talked to him and filed my report. Your input might be helpful later."

"I look forward to hearing from you Detective."

"When the men and women returned from lunch, Warren James informed them of the news he received and asked them to report any information related to the rogue trucker. By 5:30 that afternoon, they finished the order of business and adjourned. Warren looks at his watch as the group gather their papers, pens and binders. It wasn't unusual for him to work beyond that time, but tonight he was going home to have dinner with his wife at a decent hour. He looks out of the window of the second level conference room, watching the evening sun slowly sink toward the edge of the earth. It was almost Spring now. Daylight was starting to win the battle with the approaching night, spreading its rays longer and longer everyday as the winter gave way to warmer days. Warren James thought about his meeting with Sharon Landry weeks before. Thinking this might be a good time to talk about Jackson Mann, he searched for the number on his iPhone. He called her office number and reached the receptionist there, who told him that Sharon was away on business for a few days.

"Please tell her I called and ask her to return my call," said Warren James.

"I will Mr. James. Sorry, I couldn't be of more help, good night."

38

Jackson Mann was still sitting on the ground when the first Miami patrol car showed up. Two uniformed officers walked toward rocks where Josh and Bill Stood. A black sedan pulls up and stops behind the patrol car. A slightly tall, graying man stepped out and closed the door. He slips on his suit coat as he walked toward them.

"Evening boys," he said. "I don't usually like to wear this damn coat. Makes me look too damn official aside the guys," he said looking at the two officers.

"It's getting a bit chilly though, so I guess it serves a purpose right now. He said with a smile. There were crow's feet on his eyes and he wore a heavy salt and pepper mustache. The tailored blue suit he was wearing suggested he really didn't mind wearing that jacket. "I'm Detective Jack Kelly, of the New Orleans police department."

"I'm Josh Landry and this is my partner Bill Haus. We're private investigators."

"I heard you guys been chasing this fellow for a while. Well, looks like you used a phone book on him. He said with a sly smile." I can't see any marks or bruises on him anywhere."

"We didn't have to get rough, neither one of us had much left after the run we just had down the channel."

"Okay, no sense standing out here in the night. Let's take our friend into the station," said the Detective. He nodded to the officers to take Jackson Mann to the patrol car.

"Slow your roll Detective," said Josh. "Bill and I have chased this guy for several weeks now. Authorities in Missouri know we been out here, so I'm going to kind of not want to give him to you."

"So, what are we going to do with him then? You planning to take him back to Missouri?" The Detective was almost laughing. Josh and Bill didn't think it was funny.

"You got it! We are going to haul his ass back to Kansas City, said Bill. Jackson Mann looked at Josh and Bill and then back to the Detective, shaking his head.

"Well, I have to get some clearances before we can do that. I can't just turn him over to you."

"Okay, call Detective Speight in KC, he'll give you all the clearances you need. You can coordinate it with him. He'll clear us. Josh handed the Detective his cell phone with the number to Speight ready to go."

While Detective Kelly was on the phone the officers handcuffed Jackson Mann. A few minutes later, he gave the cell phone back to Josh.

"Okay, we can do this, but I need to book this man in first and properly release him to you for transport. So, we still have to go to the station."

"That works for us," said Josh.

A few hours later the New Orleans Police Department released Jackson Mann to Josh. Detective Kelly would accompany them on the journey home. They made a short stop at the hotel to gather their belongings and return the rental car. They then took ground transport to the airport where the Citation sat serviced and ready for the return to Kansas City. A twin-engine Cessna sat nearby, engines whirring. A few minutes later, a black Chevy Tahoe pulled up at the front hangar. Detective Kelly emerged from the car on the passenger side. He opened the rear door, grabbed a leather duffel bag and walked toward the plane where the three men were standing.

"I've got to say you boys go in style. That is a fine aircraft. The private investigation business must be pretty good!" said the Detective.

"Well, not exactly," said Josh. Bill owns a charter service back home. This is one of his planes. We've been friends a long time, so helps me out sometimes."

The four men climb the stairs to the cabin and buckle in for the flight. Bill at the controls and Josh shotgun in the copilot seat. The Detective and Jackson Mann sat in the seats behind them. The twin turbo fan engines whine as Bill edged the plane forward toward the man waving two orange flags, motioning the plane forward. Moments later, the Citation was thundering down the concrete, nose lifting toward the sky. As Bill banked the plane, Josh saw the Cessna had also taken off. Josh watched it while Bill finished the turn to the east. The control tower asked Bill to maintain a low elevation and speed for a moment because of air traffic. Josh could see the Cessna lagging in the distance.

"I guess that Cessna we saw on the ground is going home with us," said Josh.

"Yeah, I saw him back there, said Bill. We have to hold down the speed for now, otherwise we would have left him in the dust already."

The Citation loped along for another five minutes at low altitude. Bill could see the smaller plane pull up on the left wing about a quarter of a mile away.

"He's not supposed to be that close to us, is he?" asked Josh.

"Well, he's good so long as we both stay in our lane," said Bill.

Bill watched as the Cessna started to fall back. The plane then started to turn toward the Citation. Moments later, the plane opened fire from a small caliber gun in the nose of the plane. Bill nosed the plane down sharply just as the smaller plane crossed over the top. Detective Kelly dropped the bottle of water he was drinking. It rolled toward the front of the plane and lodged next to a fire extinguisher.

"Whoa, what the hell was that?!" said Detective Kelly.

"I'm not sure, maybe he's a friend of Mr. Mann!" said Josh.

"Yay, I guess I get to try out my new toy!" Bill said smiling.

Josh could see the Cessna circling back around toward the Citation. Bill called for clearance to increase airspeed and heading. The control tower radioed back to stand by. Ignoring the tower, Bill began a slow, gradual turn toward the Cessna.

"What are you doing man? You're heading right at him!" said the detective.

Bill leveled the plane and reached up and flipped a switch on the overhead instrument panel. A green light began flashing, followed by the sound of a door opening underneath. A second light marked *weapons* flashed.

"Wait for it", said Bill quietly. A few moments later the Cessna was coming straight at them. Bill pulled a lever on his console. The sound of machinery whirred underneath, spraying a burst of lead and fire toward the Cessna. Most of the fire was intended as a diversion, but some of it found its mark, slightly damaging the edge of the right wing of the Cessna. That was it. The smaller plane banked away and out of sight. Jackson man watched quietly as the plane disappeared in the cloudless blue sky.

"That was too easy," Bill said.

"Probably."

"You two are the craziest private investigators I have ever worked with!" said the detective.

"We try to keep things interesting," Josh said with a laugh.

"We'll probably hear from the FAA down the road," said the detective.

"Cross that bridge later," replied Josh.

39

The plane touched down at the Charles Wheeler airport in the late afternoon. Detective Sam Speight was waiting for them to take custody of Jackson Mann. Josh, Bill and detective Kelly later reported the aerial gunfire over New Orleans airspace, but Aviation authorities couldn't get verification on their report. The three men decided to just lay low on the incident until something showed up. A driver from Jet Stream arrived to take Bill to the hangar. Josh got a text message from Lace.

I'll pick you up at the airport in 15 minutes.

"It's been fun gentlemen, but I have to run." Bill said.

"Can I get a ride to the hotel, Bill?" Asked Detective Kelly.

"Sure, be glad to. How about you Josh, you riding with us?" asked Bill.

"I'm good, you guys go on. We can catch up tomorrow."

Josh watched the black Escalade make its way across the old airport parking lot and then disappear across the Broadway Bridge. It was almost the end of March and winter was nearly over. The days were beginning to reclaim the earth from the night. The nights weren't so long and dark as they were just a few weeks ago. Josh stood at the curb for a few minutes taking in the early smells of spring making its way back. The Corvette roared up to the curb. The window rolled down.

"Need a lift handsome?' said Lace.

Josh smiled, threw his bag in the rear of the car and slid down into the passenger seat. Lace looked at him with a smile filled with memories of old times. She was wearing a pair of blue denim cut jeans, and a short waisted half-zipped brown leather jacket. Josh couldn't tell for sure if Lace was wearing anything under the jacket.

"I guess you didn't need my help, huh Mr. Josh Landry?" Lace smirked.

"Sorry, things just moved so fast from day to day I wasn't quite sure when to call you. But I'm glad you're here now," said Josh. "Sharon told me you really helped us all out. You helped get the Cayman Island thing under control and we chased down Jackson Mann." You know, we've been close friends for a long time now. I think I'm just afraid of you getting hurt in my business. Guess I should know by now how you can't stay on the sideline!" said Josh.

"Yeah, I guess that's me. Thanks for saying that." Lace said softly.

"So, where are we going?" Josh asked.

"I thought we would just go to my place and have dinner. I assumed you might be tired, so I thought we could do some Italian. I made spaghetti and Cajun shrimp." Lace knew Josh would like that.

After dinner Josh lit the gas fireplace tucked in the corner of Laces flat. She took a bottle of Cabernet from a small wine rack in a corner of the granite kitchen counter. Josh opened the bottle and poured two glasses.

"Hey Josh?" said Lace, sipping the wine.

"Yeah?" Josh answered.

"We will always be friends, right?"

"Yep, always," said Josh. "Here's to us."

The wine and the flames leaping in the fireplace soon found Josh asleep on the sofa. Lace placed a blanket over him and retired to the bedroom for the evening.

40

Warren James was resting easier now that Jackson Mann was in custody. His credibility was off the hot seat for now.

"Warren, maybe you should think about retiring from this grind dear." Said Marie. "You're closing in on seventy now."

"I plan to very soon, but not until I finish cleaning up after this latest thing."

"There's always another thing, isn't there?" There's always another problem, dear. There will always be another."

"I know, but I will after this one. You'll see."

41

Josh awoke on Lace Benton's sofa. He looked at his watch. It was 5 o'clock. He quietly slipped on his shoes and pulled on his jacket. He could see Lace still asleep through her bedroom door. Josh closed it a bit and tiptoed across the carpet. He paused to right a message on a memo pad sitting on a lamp table next to the sofa.

Have to get to the Caymans. Thanks for everything.

Josh

The family laughed and shared stories on the porch of Jason and Delores' little cottage. Josh was still tired from the long flight to the Cayman, but it didn't matter. He was back with family. Savannah was smiling and happy to see her Dad, and Sharon was relieved to have Josh back safely. Madeline and Rene helped with snacks and drinks, while Jason sipped on a smooth glass of rum on ice, chatting with anyone who wanted to talk. It didn't matter. Josh thought about the cargo ship he saw pull away from the port at LaPlace.

"So how did your plan go?" asked Josh.

"You mean with Governor Lockett."

"Yeah, how did that work out?"

"Well, Governor Locket called a private meeting with Johnathan Hatch and told him he was aware of the smuggling. He told him he knew Hatch was an investor in the operation. Hatch didn't take any of it seriously and continued to publicly attack the governor. We launched two sets of media information designed to shed some negative information about Johnathan Hatch and his interest in the operation. Hatch has since gone silent."

"So that's it, you're done?"

"For now, I guess. We'll have to wait and see."

Josh hugged Sharon close and gave her a kiss on the cheek. He slept well that night, lying next to Sharon. He dreamed he was back at the old Louisiana farm back in Bayou country. He and his grandfather sat on the porch looking out over the big front yard stretching out to the bayou. It was another warm, humid evening. The sun was setting as the sound of cicadas looking for a mate began to sing.

"You ran well today, Josh," said his grandfather. "Did your family proud."

"Thanks Grandpa," said Josh.